PRAISE FOR

Lois Duncan

"**Lois Duncan is the patron saint of all things awesome.**" —Jenny Han, *New York Times* bestselling author of the To All the Boys I've Loved Before series

"Lois Duncan has always been one of my biggest inspirations. I gobbled up her novels, reading them again and again and scaring myself over and over. She's a master of suspense, so **prepare to be dazzled and spooked**!" —Sara Shepard, *New York Times* bestselling author of the Pretty Little Liars series

"I couldn't be more pleased that Lois Duncan's books will now reach **a new generation of readers**." —Judy Blume, *New York Times* bestselling author of *Forever...* and *Tiger Eyes*

"She knows what you did last summer. She knows how to find that secret evil in her characters' hearts, evil that she turns into **throat-clutching suspense** in book after book. Does anyone write scarier books than Lois Duncan? I don't think so." —R.L. Stine, *New York Times* bestselling author of the Goosebumps and Fear Street series

"There are a lot of smart authors, and a lot of authors who write reasonably well. Lois Duncan is smart, writes darn good books, and is **one of the most entertaining authors in America**."
—Walter Dean Myers, Printz Award–winning author of *Monster* and *Dope Sick*

"Lois Duncan's books kept me up many a late night reading under the covers with a flashlight!"
—Wendy Mass, author of *Leap Day* and *Heaven Looks a Lot Like the Mall*

"Haunting and suspenseful—Duncan's writing captures everything fun about reading!"
—Suzanne Young, author of *Girls with Sharp Sticks*

With slowly growing horror she stared at the letter, at the one black sentence that peered up at her from the smudged paper....

I Know What You Did
Last Summer

Also by Lois Duncan

A Gift of Magic
Daughters of Eve
Don't Look Behind You
Down a Dark Hall
Killing Mr. Griffin
Locked in Time
Stranger with My Face
Summer of Fear
The Third Eye

I KNOW WHAT YOU DID LAST SUMMER

BY LOIS DUNCAN

LITTLE, BROWN AND COMPANY
New York   Boston

Copyright © 1978 by Lois Duncan

Reader Discussion Questions and Author Q&A copyright © 2010 Hachette Book Group, Inc.
Excerpt from *Killing Mr. Griffin* copyright © 1978 by Lois Duncan

House in fog at night with window light © Lee Avison/Trevillion Images
Cover design by Sasha Illingworth and Jenny Kimura
Cover copyright © 2020 by Hachette Book Group, Inc.

Little, Brown and Company
Hachette Book Group
1290 Avenue of the Americas, New York, NY 10104
Visit us at LBYR.com

Little, Brown and Company is a division of Hachette Book Group, Inc.
The Little, Brown name and logo are trademarks of Hachette Book Group, Inc.

Originally published in hardcover by Little, Brown and Company in September 1973.
Revised Trade Paperback Edition: May 2020

The Library of Congress has cataloged the hardcover edition as follows:

Duncan, Lois, 1934—
I Know What You Did Last Summer.
Summary: Four teenagers who have desperately tried to conceal their responsibility for a hit-and-run accident are pursued by a mystery figure seeking revenge.
[1. Mystery stories] I. Title.
PZ7.D9117Iak [Fic] 73-8829
ISBN 0-316-195464 (hc) 978-0-316-09899-1 (pb)

ISBNs: 978-0-316-42535-3 (pbk.), 978-0-316-18262-1 (ebook)

Printed in the United States of America

LSC-H

Printing 2, 2021

For Ginger Palmer

CHAPTER 1

The note was there, lying beside her plate when she came down to breakfast. Later, when she thought back, Julie would remember it. Small. Plain. Her name and address hand-lettered in stark black print across the front of the envelope.

At the time, however, she had eyes only for the other letter, long and white and official. Hurriedly, she picked this up and paused, glancing across the table at her mother, who had just come in from the kitchen.

"It's here," Julie said.

"Well, aren't you going to open it?" Mrs. James set the coffeepot down on its hot plate. "You've been waiting for this long enough. I would think you'd have had it open before you even sat down."

"I guess I'm scared," Julie admitted. She slipped her forefinger under the corner of the flap. "Okay. Here goes."

Running her finger the length of the envelope, she drew out the folded sheet of stationery and smoothed it flat on the table.

"Dear Ms. James," she read aloud. "I am pleased to inform you that you have been accepted—"

"Oh, honey!" Her mother gave a little gasp of delight. "How wonderful!"

"Accepted!" Julie repeated. "Mom, can you believe it? I'm accepted! I'm going to Smith!"

Mrs. James came around the table and gave her daughter a warm hug.

"I'm so proud of you, Julie, and your dad certainly would be too. If only he could have lived to have known about it, but—oh, there's no sense in looking backward." Her eyes were suspiciously bright. "Maybe he does know. I like to think so. And if not, I'm proud enough for the both of us."

"I can't believe it," Julie said. "I honestly can't. When I took those tests, I felt as though I was missing so many questions. I guess I knew more than I thought I did."

"It's your senior year that's made this possible," her mother said. "I've never seen such a change in anybody as in you this past year. The way you've buckled down and studied—you've been a completely different person. And, I'll admit this now, it's worried me a little."

"Worried you?" Julie exclaimed in surprise. "I thought

2

you always dreamed of my going to the same college you did. Last year you were on me all the time about being out too much and never cracking a book and spending half my life at cheerleading practice."

"I know. It's just that I never expected you to do such an about-face. I can almost pinpoint the day it happened. It was just about the time you broke up with Ray."

"Mom, I've told you—" Julie tried to keep her voice light despite the sudden shock of cold that hit her stomach. "Ray and I didn't exactly break up. We just decided we were seeing too much of each other and we'd slow it down for a while. Then he left home and took off for the coast, and that took care of that."

"But to give up dating so completely "

"I haven't," Julie said impatiently. "I still go out some. In fact, Bud's coming over tonight. That's a date."

"Yes, there's Bud. But that's only been recently, and it's not the same. He's older, more serious about everything. Of course, I'm happy and proud that you've put in enough work to get accepted by a good East Coast college, but I wish you'd been able to balance it better. Somehow I have the feeling that you've missed a lot of the fun of your senior year."

"Well, you can't have it all," Julie said. Her voice sounded high and sharp, even to her own ears. The cold feeling in her stomach was spreading higher, up where it touched her heart. She shoved back her chair and got up. "I'm going up to my room. I've got to find my history notes."

"But you haven't eaten," Mrs. James exclaimed, gesturing toward the plate of scrambled eggs and toast, still untouched on the table.

"I'm sorry," Julie said. "I-I guess I'm too excited."

She could feel her mother's worried gaze upon her as she left the table. Even after she was out of eyesight, the worry stayed with her as she climbed the stairs and went down the hall to her room.

Mom knows too much, she thought. *She has this funny way of knowing more than you ever tell her.* "I've never seen such a change in anybody," her mother had said. "I can almost pinpoint the day..."

But you can't, Julie told her silently. *Not really. And you shouldn't try. Please, Mom, you shouldn't ever try.*

She entered her bedroom and shoved the door shut. It closed with a sharp click, and her mother was left behind, back down in the breakfast room with the uneaten eggs and the coffeepot. The room closed protectively around her, a perfect room for a teenage girl who was pretty and loved and happy with herself, a girl who had never had a problem.

Her mother had had the room decorated for her a little over a year ago, on her sixteenth birthday. "We'll have it done in any color you want," she had said. "You can choose."

"Pink," Julie had said immediately. It was her favorite color, the one she wore most often, even though she had red hair.

There was a pale pink T-shirt in the farthest corner of her closet, buried behind the other clothes. It had been new that night last summer. "You look like a rosebud with freckles," Ray had teased her. The shirt looked great on her, but she had never worn it after that night. She would have given it away, if she had not been afraid that her mother might remember it sometime and ask what had become of it.

Now she seated herself on the end of her bed, drawing deep, slow breaths while the cold within her faded and her heart grew still.

This is dumb, Julie told herself firmly. *It's been almost a year since the thing happened. It's over and done with, and I swore to myself I'd never think about it again. If I let myself get this uptight over some innocent little comment of Mom's, I'll wind up right back where I started, an absolute basket case.*

Across from her in the oval mirror over the bureau another Julie looked back at her, pale and unsmiling. *I have changed,* she thought with mild surprise. The girl in the mirror bore little resemblance to last year's Julie, bubbly, bouncy, spark plug of the pep squad, the cheerleader with the smallest size and the biggest yell. This girl had shadows behind her eyes and a tightness about the mouth.

You're going to Smith, Julie told herself. *Just keep that in mind, will you? You're getting out of here in only a couple of months. You won't be going to the university, you'll be going east, away from this town, and the road, and the picnic area above it. You won't be running into Ray's mother at the drugstore. You won't see Barry on campus or Helen on television. You'll be out —free! A new place, new people, new things to do and think about, a whole new set of things to remember.*

5

She felt steadier now. Her breathing was slow again and even. She picked up the letter from Smith, which she had dropped on the bed beside her, and looked again at her name, neatly typed, on the official-looking envelope. She would take it to school with her, she decided; there were people there she could show it to. Not to any other students, especially—there wasn't anyone she was that close to this year—but Mr. Price, her English teacher, would be happy for her, and Mrs. Busby, who taught American Studies.

And tonight when Bud came over she would show it to him. He'd be impressed, and sorry, maybe, because she would be going away. Bud had been calling so often recently that it was possible he was getting more serious than he should be. It would be good for him to realize that this relationship wasn't going to go anywhere, that it was just for now and in the fall she would be somewhere else.

There was a rap on the bedroom door.

"Julie?" her mother asked. "Are you keeping track of time, dear?"

"Yes. No...I guess I wasn't." Julie got up off the bed and opened the door. "I was just sitting here, gloating over the acceptance. Honestly, I'd just about given up hoping. It's been so long since I applied."

"I know," Mrs. James said sympathetically. "And I didn't mean to take the wind out of your sails by criticizing. I know how hard you've been working, and I've just been afraid you were overdoing it. I'm glad that now you can relax and enjoy your summer."

"I'm glad too," Julie said.

She put her arms around her mother and gave her an impulsive hug. Her mother's arms came back around her, surprised and glad.

I ought to hug her more often, Julie thought. *I don't deserve to have somebody like this for a mother. I love her so much, and I'm all she has since Daddy died. Now I'll be going away and she'll be alone, and still she's happy for me.*

"Are you sure you'll be okay?" she asked against her mother's soft cheek. "Can you get along, do you think, with me so far away?"

"Oh, I think so," Mrs. James said with a catch in her voice that was supposed to pass for laughter. "I made out all right before you were born, didn't I? I'll keep busy. I've been thinking that maybe I'll go back to work full time."

"Would you like that?" Julie asked. Her mother had been a home economics teacher before her marriage, and since her husband's death eight years ago, she had been working as a substitute.

"I think I would. It would be nice to have my own class again. With you out of the nest there won't be anyone to need me at home, so it's time to be needed somewhere else."

"I did lose track of time," Julie said apologetically. "I'd better get going."

Her mother glanced at her watch. "You are late. Would you like for me to drive you?"

"That's all right," Julie told her. "I haven't been late all year, so it won't kill me to get a late slip today. And maybe I

7

won't. Mr. Price is a pretty nice guy about things like that."

She gathered up her books and history notes from the bedside table. Downstairs she paused long enough to rummage in the coin bowl on the sideboard for enough money to buy a Coke later.

"I'll see you after school," she said. "Bud's not picking me up till around eight, so there's no reason we have to eat early. Are you going out anyplace?"

"I don't have any plans," Mrs. James said. "Wait a minute, honey. You didn't get your letter."

"Yes, I did. It's here in my notebook."

"No, I mean the other one." Her mother leaned across the table to pick up the second envelope, half-concealed by the edge of the egg plate. "There were two pieces of mail for you this morning. Not that this could possibly be as exciting as the first one."

"It's the size of a party invitation, though I don't know who would be inviting me to a party." Julie took the small envelope from her mother's hand. "That's funny. It has big block printing and no return address."

She tore the envelope open and removed a folded sheet of lined paper.

"Who is it from?" her mother called back over her shoulder as she carried the breakfast dishes into the kitchen. "Anybody I've ever heard of?"

"No," Julie said. "Nobody you know."

With slowly growing horror she stared at the letter, at the

one black sentence that peered up at her from the smudged paper.

I'm going to be sick, she thought. Her legs felt weak, and she reached out and caught hold of the edge of the table to steady herself.

It's a dream, she told herself hopefully. *I'm not really awake and standing here in the dining room at all. I'm lying in bed upstairs, asleep, and this is only a nightmare like the ones I used to have back in the beginning. I'll close my eyes, and when I open them I will wake up. It will be gone . . . the paper will be gone. It will never have been.*

So she closed her eyes, and when she opened them again the paper was still there in her hand with one short sentence printed on it:

I KNOW WHAT YOU DID LAST SUMMER.

CHAPTER 2

It was almost dusk when Barry Cox pulled out of the parking area behind the frat house and drove through the campus and then north on Madison to the Four Seasons Apartments.

It was a familiar drive; in fact, he sometimes said jokingly to his frat brothers that the car knew it so well that it could drive there by itself.

"Sure it won't get confused?" they joked back. "It knows the way to a couple of other pads too."

"It keeps them straight," Barry told them smugly. "It's got a GPS."

It was true that Helen wasn't the only girl Barry went out with, though he was pretty sure that he was the only guy she was seeing. Crazy too, because living where she did, in an apartment complex full of singles, and looking like a swimsuit model, and holding her showy job—well, there were bound to be plenty of werewolves howling under her window.

That was one reason he continued seeing her on a regular basis. He hadn't planned to once high school was over. A college man had a wide territory, and there were some pretty hot girls on the University campus who would be easy to hook up with, no strings attached. Then, when Helen had been handed that job as Future Star, it had changed things. A guy would have to be nuts to throw over the Channel Five Future Star.

Now as he pulled into the Four Seasons parking lot, he grinned to himself. Helen was doing all right for an eighteen-year-old who hadn't even finished high school. His mother had gone through the ceiling when she learned about Helen's dropping out at the end of her junior year. "It proves what I've said from the beginning," she had told him. "A person is the result of her background. That girl isn't your kind, Barry; I don't understand how you ever started dating her."

Which, of course, was part of the reason—he knew it would bug his mother. And then there were her looks. Helen was beauty queen material, and the fact was already beginning to pay off for her. Not many girls her age had their own apartments without even having to split the cost with a roommate. Helen's older sister, Elsa, was still living at home, stashing away half her earnings as a cashier in a department store, hoping that maybe someday, in a year or so, she might be able to make the break and get her own little hole-in-the-wall. And

11

here was Helen with her own car, trendy clothes, anything she wanted, and not a worry in the world.

So what had she been so upset about on the phone? That call had surprised him. Helen wasn't like a lot of girls, always calling their boyfriends. She seldom even texted him unless there was a definite reason.

This time she hadn't given one.

"I've got to see you," she had said. "It's important. Can you come over later when I get off work?"

"Tonight? Heller, we were just out last night. You know this week is off limits. I've got finals to study for."

"I told you, it's important." There had been an edge to her voice, something that didn't happen often with Helen. Usually if he told her something, she accepted it without question. "I wouldn't call you like this if it wasn't. You know that."

"Can't you tell me what it's about?"

"No." She had left it at that. Just a flat no. He was intrigued in spite of himself. He did have exams to study for, and he had a date later for coffee with Ashley Something-or-other from the Tri-Delt house, but nothing that couldn't be shoved over a little.

"Well, if we make it early," he said. "Right after dinner."

"That's fine. The earlier the better." She hadn't asked him to eat with her, and he was fine with that. Those domestic evenings with Helen running around serving pot roast by candlelight were rough to handle. He knew what she was aiming for, and it wasn't what he was aiming for, and the whole game was making him jittery.

"I'm calling from the studio," she said. "I've got a webcast to do in a couple of minutes. I'll see you around seven then, okay?"

"Okay," Barry had said.

The conversation had left him curious. So curious, in fact, that he hadn't bothered to go to the dining hall for dinner. He had just stopped at a Wendy's and picked up a couple of burgers and a Frosty. Now here it was, barely past six-thirty, and he was climbing out of his car and starting up the walk that led past the pool to the steps to the second-level apartments.

The pool and the area around it were crowded. The spring evening was still pretty cool, but the pool itself was heated, and there were some polar bear types splashing around and plenty of pretty girls sitting high and dry in deck chairs, taking the first opportunity of the season to show off their figures in bikinis.

For a moment he stopped, just enjoying the view, a little surprised that Helen wasn't among them. She had a figure that was better than the best of them, and she wasn't one who minded displaying it.

"Hi," called one of the girls, a shapely little brunette in a red and white halter and short shorts. "Are you looking for an apartment? There's a vacancy on the second floor."

"Nope," Barry replied, giving her a measuring glance. "Not this year, anyway."

Actually, he would have given anything to be able to live in a place like this, but it wasn't his mother's idea of something the old man should finance. He was damned lucky, when it came to that, just to have gotten into a frat house.

He went on around the pool and up the stairs, pausing to glance back at the brunette, who had turned sideways in her chair and was still watching him. Then he went on down the upper deck and rapped on the door of Helen's apartment.

He had to wait a few minutes for his knock to be answered, something that seldom happened at Helen's. Then the door opened and she was standing before him. She looked good, as always. Her honey-colored hair was pulled back from her face and held in place with a gold band, and her violet eyes were carefully shadowed and outlined to make them even lovelier. She was wearing pale blue pants and a silk blouse with a chunky crystal necklace at the throat; evidently she had not changed clothes since coming back from the studio.

"Good," she said. "You're early. I was hoping you might be."

"I'm glad I didn't disappoint you." Something was wrong, Barry decided. Something was decidedly strange; this wasn't the way he was usually greeted. "What's up, anyway?"

"Come on in," Helen said. "We can't talk here."

He stepped through the doorway and knew instinctively that someone else was in the apartment. He glanced at Helen questioningly.

"Who's here?"

"Julie. Julie James."

"You've got to be kidding!" He followed Helen into the living room where the other girl was seated on the sofa. "Hi,

14

Julie. Long time, no see. How is everything going?"

"Hello, Barry," Julie said stiffly.

She wasn't as cute as he remembered her, that was for certain. Not that she had ever been the beauty that Helen was, but she had always had enough sparkle so that the lack of real looks went unnoticed. Now that glow seemed to have faded. Her eyes looked huge in a face that was too small to hold them.

"Well, hi," Barry said again. "It's good to see you. I thought you'd kind of dropped us off your friend list."

"I came here for a reason." Julie's eyes went past him to Helen. "You didn't tell him?"

"No," Helen said. "I thought you ought to be the one. It's your letter."

"What are you talking about?" Barry asked them impatiently. "What's the big secret?"

"It isn't a secret," Julie said shortly. She gestured toward a sheet of notebook paper that was lying on the coffee table.

For a moment Barry gazed at it unseeingly. Then the words took shape for him, and he felt his breath catch in his throat.

"Where did that come from?"

"It came in the mail this morning," Julie told him. "It was just there, stuck in with a lot of other letters. There wasn't any return address."

"'I know what you did—'" Barry began to read the statement aloud. "That's crazy! Who would send you something like that?"

"I don't know," Julie said again. "It was just there."

15

"Have you mentioned anything to anybody? Is there somebody who would know?"

"I haven't said a thing."

"Helen?" He glanced across at her. Her delicate, fine-boned face looked as bewildered as Julie's. "Nobody. I haven't said a word to anybody either."

"Well, neither have I. We made the pact, didn't we? So there's no way this has any meaning. It's some joke, somebody taking a jab at Julie."

They were silent a moment. Shouts and laughter drifted up from the swimming pool through the open window. For a fleeting second the brunette in the red and white shorts slid through Barry's mind.

I wish I were out there, he thought, *with a beer in one hand, just kidding around with the bunch of them. If there's one thing I don't need, it's to deal with a scene like this.*

"It must have been Ray," he said. "There's nobody else it could be. Ray wrote it as some kind of joke."

"He wouldn't," Julie said. "You know he wouldn't do that."

"I don't know anything of the kind. You dumped that guy pretty abruptly, you know. One day you two were an item and the next you didn't even want to talk to him. This could be his way of getting back at you by shaking you up a little."

"Ray wouldn't do that. Besides," she motioned toward the envelope that was lying beside the letter, "this was postmarked from here. The last card I had from Ray was sent from California."

"No." Helen spoke up suddenly. "Ray's back in town. I saw him yesterday."

"You did?" Julie turned to her in astonishment. "Where?"

"In that little deli across from the studio at lunch time. He was coming out as I went in. I almost didn't recognize him, he's changed so much. He's real tan now and he's grown a beard. Then I looked back, and he was looking back too, and it was definitely Ray. He held up his hand and kind of waved at me."

"Then that's who it must be," Barry said. "Of all the sick tricks! The guy must have gone over the edge."

"I don't believe it," Julie said decidedly. "I know Ray better than either of you, and he wouldn't do a thing like this. He felt worse than any of us when...*it* happened. He wouldn't make a joke of it this way."

"I don't think he would either," agreed Helen. She reached over and turned the paper so that she could see it better. "Is there any other way someone could have found out? Maybe by tracing the car?"

"Not a chance," Barry said. "Ray and I spent a whole day hammering the dent out of that fender. Then we painted the car and got rid of it the next weekend."

"Julie, are you sure you haven't said anything?" Helen asked her. "I know how close you are to your mother."

"I told you, I didn't," Julie said. "And if I did tell Mom, do you think she'd mail me something like this?"

"No," Helen admitted. "It's just that there doesn't seem to be any answer besides that. If none of us told, if it wasn't the car—"

"Did it ever occur to the two of you," Barry broke in, "that this note might be about something else entirely?"

"About something else?" Julie repeated blankly.

"It doesn't actually say anything, does it?"

"It says, 'I know what you did—'"

"So? Last summer was three months long, you know. You probably did plenty of things."

"You know what it means."

"No, I don't, and neither do you. Maybe the person who wrote it doesn't know either. Maybe it's a joke. You know how kids are sometimes, making crank calls and writing notes to people and sending spam. So some kid decides to play a prank—he writes a dozen of these and sends them to strangers right out of the phone book. Do you think there's a person in the world who, getting a message like this, couldn't look back and think of something he did last summer that he wasn't proud of?"

Julie digested the argument in silence. Then she said, "But we have an unlisted phone number."

"Well, then, he found you some other way. Maybe it's a nerd from school who has a thing for you and wants to get a reaction. Or some guy you pissed off because you wouldn't go out with him, or the kid who packs bags at the grocery store. There are plenty of creeps in the world who get their kicks out of getting girls all shook up."

"Barry's right about that, Julie." There was relief in Helen's voice. "I've known some people like that myself. You wouldn't believe the phone calls you get when you work on television! There was one guy who used to call me, and he wouldn't say a word. He'd just breathe. I was ready to go out of my mind. I'd answer the phone, thinking maybe it was Barry, and there would just be this heavy breathing in my ear."

"Well," Julie said slowly, "I suppose that's possible. I-I never thought about something like that."

"If the thing last summer hadn't happened, if you'd gotten this note and there wasn't something that came straight into your mind, you'd have thought about it, wouldn't you?"

"Maybe. Yes, I guess I would have." She drew a long breath. "Do you really think that's it? It's just somebody's idea of a joke?"

"Sure," Barry told her firmly. "What else could it be? Look, if somebody did know something, he wouldn't be writing silly notes, would he? He'd go to the police."

"And it wouldn't be now," Helen said. "It would have been back last July when the thing actually happened. Why would anybody wait ten months to react?"

"I don't know," Julie said. "When you put it that way, it doesn't sound likely."

"It isn't likely," said Barry. "You've got yourself all tied up in knots over nothing. And Heller, you're just as bad, calling

19

me like that. You had me thinking something awful had happened."

"I'm sorry," Helen said contritely. "Julie called me about it this afternoon, and I reacted the same way she did. We both panicked."

"Well, un-panic," Barry told her. He got to his feet. Helen's lovely apartment, which always before had seemed so spacious and luxurious, was suddenly unbearably suffocating. "I've got to get going."

"Why don't you stay awhile?" Helen suggested. "I've got a whole hour and a half before I have to leave for the studio."

"That's an hour and a half that I don't have. I told you this was a closed week and I have to study." He turned to Julie. "Do you need a ride? I can drop you off at your house on my way back to the campus."

"No, thanks," Julie said. "I don't need a ride. I've got Mom's car."

"Don't you want to stay, Julie?" Helen asked her. "We haven't talked for ages. There must be a lot for us to catch up on."

"Another time, okay? I've got a date picking me up at eight."

"Take it easy, then," Barry said. "It was good seeing you." He turned back to Helen. "I'll be seeing you, Heller."

"Do you want to plan on doing something Monday?" Helen suggested. "It's Memorial Day, which usually means a party of some kind around this place."

"It depends on how much studying I get done over the weekend. I'll call you. I promise."

She started to get up to walk him to the door, but he waved her back down. The last thing he felt like after this was an affectionate farewell scene with Julie as an audience.

He let himself out, leaving the two girls together, and went down the steps and back along the side of the pool. The underwater lights were on now, and the crowd of exhibitionists had thinned a little. The perpetual party that always started around the pool on Friday evenings had broken, as it generally did, into several smaller parties, most of which had moved upstairs into private apartments.

Gaslights flickered along the walkway, and the greenery in the planters rustled slightly in the faint evening breeze. Barry got into his car and turned the key in the ignition.

Somewhere in the parking lot another engine came to life. Sitting quiet, Barry let the motor idle. There was no movement that he could see among the rows of parked cars.

Coincidence, Barry told himself impatiently. *I'm as uptight as those crazy girls.*

He flicked on the headlights, threw the car into gear, and pulled out of the lot onto Madison Avenue. He drove slowly back to the campus, glancing occasionally into the rearview mirror. There were lights behind him, but then it was early on a weekend evening, a time when streets were always busy with traffic.

When he turned onto Campus Drive the car behind him turned as well, but when he slowed and pulled over to the curb, it went on past him without hesitation and disappeared around a curve at the end of the street.

Crazy, Barry repeated to himself. *Why should I suddenly start thinking people are following me just because Julie James pushes the panic button? Like I told her, there are all kinds of creeps in the world.*

But he kept having the uneasy feeling that there was a pair of eyes boring into his back right between the shoulder blades when he left the car in the lot and walked back across the lawn to the entrance of the frat house.

CHAPTER 3

There was a car parked in front of the James' house when Julie pulled into the driveway. Her first thought was that Bud had come early, but a second glance told her that this was not Bud's cream-colored Dodge.

The front door of the house stood open, and through the screen voices floated to her as she crossed the lawn and mounted the steps to the front porch. One voice was her mother's, lifted with unaccustomed gaiety.

The second voice stopped her. For a long moment Julie stood frozen, caught and held, unmoving. Then her mother, who was seated on the far side of the living room, facing the doorway, glanced up and saw her.

"Julie, look who's here! It's Ray!"

Julie opened the screen and went into the room, drawing the solid door closed behind her.

"Hi," she said a bit stiffly. "I saw the car outside but I didn't recognize it."

"It's my dad's," Raymond Bronson said, getting to his feet. He stood there awkwardly, as though wondering what sort of greeting to offer. Then he held out his hand. "How are you, Jules?"

"Okay," Julie said. "Fine." She went forward and put her hand in his, holding it formally, then releasing it. It was a harder hand than she remembered. "I didn't know you were back. Your last card was from the coast. You said you were working on some kind of fishing boat."

"I was," Ray said. "The guy who owns the boat has a kid who works with him in the summers. There wasn't room for both of us."

"That's too bad," Julie said, because she could think of nothing else to say.

"Not really. Jobs like that are on-again, off-again. I was about ready to come home for awhile anyway." He was waiting for her to sit down, so she did. Not beside him on the sofa, but in the armchair facing him. He took his seat again. "Your mom's been telling me about your getting your go-ahead from Smith. That's great. You must really have been hitting the books."

"She has," Mrs. James said with pride. "You wouldn't have known her this year, Ray. I don't know whether it's because you haven't been here to keep her out half the night or whether

24

she just suddenly decided to buckle down, but the results have been remarkable."

"That's great," Ray said again.

Mrs. James rose. "I've got a cake waiting to be iced in the kitchen, and I know you kids have a lot of catching up to do. I'll bring you out a piece when I get it done."

"I can't stay long," Ray said.

"I have a date," said Julie, "in just a few minutes."

She didn't meet his eyes when she said it, although she knew, of course, that he would probably expect her to have a date on a Friday night. He had undoubtedly done his own share of socializing out in California. She wondered what he would think of Bud. Bud was so far from the type of boy she had dated in school, so far from Ray's type, though Ray himself had changed tremendously since she had last seen him. He looked older. He was very tan; his light hair grew thick and long down over his ears, and his brows were bleached pale over his cat-green eyes. As Helen had reported earlier, he had grown a beard. It was short and stubby and looked as though it belonged on somebody else's face.

They sat in awkward silence after Mrs. James left the room. Then they both spoke at once.

"It's nice that you—" Julie began, and Ray said, "I just thought—" They both stopped speaking. Then Julie said carefully, "It's nice that you came by."

"I thought I'd say hello," said Ray. "I've thought about you a lot. I-I just wanted to see how you were."

"I'm fine," Julie repeated, and the green eyes that knew her so well, that had seen her through so many situations — through parties and picnics and cheerleading tryouts, and being caught cheating on a math test, and coming down with a rare case of the chicken pox right before Homecoming — those eyes kept looking in disbelief.

"You don't look fine," Ray said. "You look like hell. Has it been dragging on you like this ever since?"

"No," Julie said. "I don't think about it."

"I don't believe you."

"I don't," Julie told him. "I don't let myself." She lowered her voice. "I made up my mind right after the funeral. I knew if I kept thinking... well, what good would that have done? People go crazy dwelling on things they can't change." She paused. "I sent him flowers."

Ray looked surprised. "You did?"

"I went down to People's Flower Shoppe and bought some yellow roses. I had them delivered without my name on them. I know it was silly. It couldn't help. It was just... I felt I had to do something and I couldn't think of anything else."

"I know," Ray said. "I felt the same way. I didn't think about sending flowers. I kept waking up at night and seeing that curve in the road again, that bicycle coming up suddenly out of the dark like that, and I'd feel the thud and then the bump as the wheels went over it. I'd lie there and shake."

"That's why you went away." It was a statement, not a question.

"Isn't that why you're going to Smith? To get away from here? You've never cared that much about college. You used to talk about maybe taking computer courses or something right here in town while I went to the University. Going east to school was the last thing you had on your mind."

"Barry's at the U now," Julie said. "He's on the football team."

"I saw Helen yesterday at lunch. She looked pretty."

"She's a Future Star," Julie said. "Did you know? Channel Five had this beauty contest thing based on photographs, and Helen won it. She's got a full-time job representing the station for all kinds of things, giving spot announcements and small news reports. She even deejays her own webcast in the afternoons."

"Great," Ray said. "Are they still together?"

"I guess so. I saw them today." Julie shook her head. "I don't know how Helen can do it—keep going with him, I mean. She was there, she saw him that night, she heard the things he said. How can she still think he's so wonderful? How can she even stand to have him touch her?"

"It was an accident," Ray reminded her. "God knows, Barry didn't plan it. It could have been me driving the car. It would have been if I hadn't won the toss for the back seat."

"But you would have stopped," Julie said.

There was a long silence as the words hung there between them.

"Would I?" Ray asked at last.

"Of course," Julie said sharply. And then, "Wouldn't you?"

"Who knows?" Ray shrugged his shoulders. "I tell myself I would have. You think I would have. But how can we know? How can you know how anybody's going to react in a situation like that? We'd all had a few beers and smoked a little pot. It happened so fast."

"You called for the ambulance. You wanted to go back."

"But I didn't insist on it. You wanted to go back too, but we didn't. We let Barry talk us into the pact. I could have held out, but I didn't. I must have wanted to be talked into it. I'm no better than Barry, Jules, so don't try to make him the black knight and me the prince on the white horse. It just isn't that way."

"You're as bad as Helen," Julie said. "The both of you! You form the Great Society for Admiring Barry Cox. You'd stick up for him no matter what he did. You should have heard her tonight, begging him to call her this weekend, and here they are, supposedly a couple. It's just so degrading."

"I don't see anything degrading about sticking by your guy if you care about him." Ray's brows drew together in that quizzical look she knew so well. "What were you doing at Helen's anyway? I thought you'd burned all your bridges, that you were cutting ties with all of us."

"I have," Julie told him. "That is, I meant to. Today I got a letter in the mail. It upset me and I called Helen, and then she called Barry, and suddenly there we all were, hashing it over. I wish now I'd just chucked it and not made such a big deal about it."

Ray looked interested. "What sort of letter?"

"Just a prank thing. Helen says she gets them sometimes, and phone calls and e-mail too, but I never got any before, so I overreacted." She opened her purse and fished out the envelope. "Here it is, if you want to see it."

Ray got up and came over and sat on the arm of her chair, taking the letter out of her hand. He opened it and read it.

"Barry thinks it was written by some kid," Julie said. "That it doesn't really mean anything, it just happened to have hit on something that struck a nerve." She paused, watching his face as he studied the black line of printing. "Is that what you think?"

"It's possible," Ray said, "but it's one hell of a coincidence. Why pick on you? Do you know anybody who could have sent it?"

"Barry thought maybe some boy from school."

"You said you're dating." He raised his eyes from the paper. "This guy you're going out with tonight, is he the practical joker type?"

"As far from it as you can get," said Julie. "Bud's a nice guy. Older. Serious about everything. He was in the army and fought in Iraq. The last thing he'd ever do is write silly notes."

"Are you in love with him?" The question was so sudden, so far away from the previous discussion, that she was unprepared.

29

"No," she said.

"But he is with you?"

"I don't think so. Maybe a little. Please, Ray, this is just a nice guy I met one day in the library. He asked me out and Mom had been bugging me about never going anywhere anymore, so I went. And then it was easy just to keep on. Besides, what difference does it make to you? You and I—we're not a thing anymore."

"Aren't we?" He reached out a hand and placed it gently under her chin, tilting her face up so that it was raised to his. The face that looked down at her was familiar, darker and stronger than she remembered it, framed with shaggy hair and a beard. But the eyes were the same. No stranger could ever look at her through Ray's green eyes.

"It's still there," he said. "You know it is. You could feel it, just the way I could, the moment you walked into the room. We had too good a thing for too long. We can't just let it go."

"That's how it has to be," Julie said. "I mean it, Ray. I really do. It's the only way we'll ever forget. I'm going to leave here, leave all the people and places connected with that horrible night, and never look back. It's over and done with. There's no repairing it. So I'm going to erase it."

"And you think that's possible?" His voice was sad. "Sweetie, something like that doesn't get erased. I thought maybe it could be too, there in the beginning. That's why I packed up and took off. New places, new people...I thought that would do it. But it didn't. You can't run away. You at

Smith, me out in California, it's still there with us. I realized that finally. It's why I came home."

"If you can't run away," Julie said chokingly, "what can you do?"

"Face up to it."

"You mean, break the pact?"

"No," Ray said. "We can't do that. But we can talk to the others. We can dissolve the pact, if we're all in agreement."

"Never. Barry will never agree to it, and if he won't, Helen won't."

The doorbell rang.

Ray's hand dropped to his side. He got up from the arm of her chair. "That must be your friend."

"I guess so. He was picking me up at eight." Julie's eyes went nervously from Ray's face to the door.

"Don't worry, I'll behave myself. I'll probably even like him. He's got good taste in girls, anyway."

They went to the door together, and Julie introduced them.

Bud said, "Raymond Bronson? You any relation to Booter Bronson who runs the sporting goods store?"

"His son," Ray told him. "I hear you just got back from Iraq. I sure don't envy you that gig."

They shook hands civilly and stood and talked a few moments in a pleasant fashion, as though they might have been friends if given the chance. Then Ray left, and Julie excused herself and went upstairs to comb her hair.

31

When she came down, Bud was still standing there by the door as he had been when she left him. He looked up at her and smiled as she came down the stairs, and for an instant she felt like crying because his smile was such a nice one and because his eyes weren't green.

CHAPTER 4

One of the pleasant things about being the Channel Five Future Star, Helen Rivers often reminded herself, was the hours. Eleven o'clock in the morning usually found her stretched in a deck chair, soaking up sunshine beside the swimming pool. Because this particular day happened to be Saturday, it was not exactly her private pool; an assortment of schoolteachers used it also. But on the usual weekday she could sleep half the morning and come down to find that she had the whole lovely area to herself.

"I can't imagine why they pay you all that money," her sister Elsa sometimes commented on those weekends when Helen went dutifully home for Sunday dinner. "You don't do anything that anyone else couldn't do—just smile and play songs and make silly comments."

Elsa worked an eight-hour day at Wards Department Store and was a great believer that the only kind of work that counted was the kind that made your back ache and sent you home exhausted.

"Oh, there's more to it than that," Helen tried to tell her. "You're at their beck and call whenever they need somebody to represent the station for publicity reasons. And it can really kill your evenings, having to give reports on the ten o'clock news."

Even to her own ears the statement sounded ludicrous. In all honesty she knew that being selected as the Channel Five Future Star was the culmination of almost every dream she had ever had.

Helen's looks were the best thing she had going for her, and she was born realistic enough to have recognized the fact early. At the age of twelve she had sat down one day and examined herself in the mirror.

What she had seen there had been pleasing, but not pleasing enough. Cold-bloodedly she had analyzed her attributes: good bones, even teeth, fine features. She had a nice chest for her age but too much weight in the hips. Her coloring was too pale, her hair rather ordinary, but thick and healthy. Her hands were not particularly small, but they were long-fingered and artistic-looking, despite bitten fingernails.

She broke the fingernail habit immediately through sheer willpower. The rest took more time, especially the weight loss. Helen liked to eat, and the food that was served in her family's home was usually of the inexpensive and starchy variety. A strenuous diet had brought her figure under control, and experimentation with rinses and makeup had brought out the honey highlights in her hair and fringed her deep violet eyes, her most unusual feature, with long, blue-black lashes.

"What do you think you are, a fairy princess?" Elsa had taunted her.

Helen had ignored her. It would have been nice, she had admitted to herself, if such had been the case. As the second daughter in a large family, she had no illusions about magic and fairy godmothers. She had only to look at her own mother, haggard from years of housework and budget-stretching and childbearing, and her father, sweating out his days at construction work, to know that her chances for a luxurious future were slim.

Still, she was pretty, and that could serve for something. *It would have to,* she told herself, because she certainly had no academic talents. Dropping out of school to accept the offer of the Future Star job had been more of a relief than a sacrifice. She had stuck through school that far for one reason only — she had fallen in love.

She had loved Barry Cox from the first moment she had seen him. Big and broad-shouldered, handsome and popular, he was as close to perfect as any guy she could ever have imagined. As captain of the city's winning high school football team, he could have had his pick of any girl he wanted. His choosing her was the surprising thing, the actual miracle.

35

It had happened so suddenly that she had never been able to figure out the exact circumstances. She had been walking home from school when a bright red sports car had pulled up beside her, and Barry had been in it.

"Hi, there," he had said. "Climb in and I'll drive you home."

When he dropped her off, he had asked her for a date. It had happened that simply, and her world had never been the same again.

Now, stretched in the deck chair, letting the warmth of the morning sun sink into her body, she thought, *I shouldn't have called him.*

Barry didn't like to be pressured. She had learned that from his mother. One time soon after they had started dating, before she knew his cell number, she had called him at home to check on what time he was coming to pick her up.

Mrs. Cox had answered the phone.

"Let me give you some advice, dear," she had said in her cool, sharp voice. "Barry is a boy who doesn't react well to being chased. If he wants to talk with you, he will do the calling. Your little affair will last longer that way, believe me."

Since then, she had called him only when absolutely necessary. Yesterday's call had seemed at the time to fall into that category, but in retrospect she realized that it had not. Barry had been irritated; he did have exams to study for. Dragging him away from his books to confront him with that silly note had been ridiculous. His explanation had been so reasonable

36

that it now seemed incredible that she and Julie could not have thought of it themselves.

"Excuse me. Would it be all right if I sat down here?" The voice came from directly beside her, startling her so that she jumped. Her eyes flew open and for a moment she was blinded by the sun.

"I'm sorry," the young man said. "I didn't mean to scare you."

"You didn't. I must have been half asleep. I didn't hear you come up."

Helen shaded her eyes with one hand to look up at him. Her glance took in the brown eyes, brown hair, a strong, square-cut face, a medium sort of build. He was wearing olive green swimming trunks, cut like shorts.

Helen was used to the faces around the apartment complex, and this one was unfamiliar.

"You're new here?" she asked.

"Just moved in yesterday. Apartment 211. Will it bother you if I sit down?"

"No, of course not." Helen leaned back in the chair and watched idly as he settled himself into an identical chair beside her. There were plenty of other seats around the pool and a number of other people beside whom he could have sat.

"This is the heavy day for sunbathers," she told him. "Saturdays most people are off from work and trying to build up their tans. My name's Helen Rivers."

"Collingsworth Wilson, if you'll excuse the mouthful.

37

Just out of the service. I've been staying out at my folks' place in the mountains and finally decided to cut loose and get my own apartment. I think I'll be going to summer school at the University."

"The guy I go with goes to the U," Helen said. She made a point of working such a statement into the conversation as soon as possible upon meeting new people. She had found that it allowed the pleasure of harmless flirtation without presenting the problem of having to reject overtures. "Collingsworth is a different sort of name. Do they call you Collie?"

"I've got a family nickname that my kid brother stuck me with," the boy told her. "But Collie's okay too. A lot of people do call me that. I'm like a well-trained puppy; I answer to anything."

"A well-trained Collie?" Helen said, smiling. She was not usually much on puns, but this one had been too easy. "I'm glad to meet you. We're practically next-door neighbors. I'm on the second level too, down the way from you in 215."

"And who's the boyfriend?" Collie asked. "I want to be sure to avoid him."

"His name's Barry Cox. He lives on campus, but he comes over a lot. You'll be meeting him. Everybody meets everybody here in the summer." She closed her eyes again and rolled over onto her stomach so that the sun could reach her shoulders. "The pool area makes a wonderful meeting place. We all sit around and talk and party. Four Seasons is a great place to live. I know you'll like it."

"I like it already," Collie said simply. "But I'd like it even better if the prettiest girl here wasn't all tied up to some jerk before I can even get my bid in. Have you been hooked up with this guy long?"

"Almost two years. We were steadies back in high school, and he's definitely not a jerk. Do you think I'm burning?"

"I don't know," Collie said. "I can't tell what's happening under all that suntan lotion."

"Well, I'd better get inside. I've been out here a couple of hours already." Helen rolled over and sat up. "I can't afford to start peeling. If I look a mess I might lose my job."

"What sort of work do you do where you can't get a sunburn?" Collie asked. "Are you a model or something?"

"I'm the Channel Five Future Star." Despite herself, Helen could not keep the pride from showing in her voice. It was still such a new sensation to be able to make such a statement. "Maybe you've seen me on TV."

"If I had, I'm sure I'd remember it," the boy said seriously. "I don't usually watch TV much, but I can see where I'm going to have to start."

"There's a big screen down in the common area," Helen told him. She picked up the bottle of suntan lotion and got to her feet.

He'll be a nice addition to the men around here, she thought objectively. *He's not as handsome as Barry by a long shot, but a lot of girls are going to like him. Wait till those two man-hungry schoolteachers in 214 get a look at him. They'll tear each other to shreds over who gets her hooks in first.*

"Enjoy the sun," she said. "But don't doze off the way I did or you might find yourself turned into a lobster. This southwest sun can really get to you when you're not used to it."

"Got it. Good luck on not peeling." Collingsworth Wilson raised a hand in casual farewell.

He's nice, Helen thought again as she skirted the pool and climbed the stairs to the second level. The doors to the second-floor apartments all opened onto a narrow balcony. She walked slowly along it, wondering how red she really was. It had been a foolish thing, she knew, to lie out like that right in the middle of the day. A tan could look great on camera, but it had to be picked up carefully at no more than an hour at a time.

If I do peel, she told herself, *maybe I can work it into a report on the weather.* "It was good and hot today. I hope you viewers showed better sense than I did." That was the sort of thing she was beginning to learn to do, to toss out ad libs. As she kept telling Elsa, there was more to television work than just looking pretty and smiling. You had to think under stress and seem natural and come out with occasional quirky remarks so you didn't come across as a mechanical doll.

There was a paper taped to the door of her apartment. She didn't see it until she reached it, and then she could only stand and stare.

It was a picture cut from a magazine ad. The text had been cut away, and what remained was the image of a little boy on a bicycle.

CHAPTER 5

When the envelope arrived in the morning mail, Ray Bronson was not surprised. He opened it and drew out the newspaper clipping. He knew what it contained, for he had read it many times before. Now he did so again and felt all the old sensations:

"A ten-year-old boy was killed last night in a hit-and-run accident on Mountain Road, two miles south of the Silver Springs picnic area. Dead is Daniel Gregg, son of Michael and Mary Gregg of 1279 Morningside Road Northeast. Daniel was riding his bicycle when he was struck by an unidentified vehicle.

"A phone call from an alleged occupant of that vehicle informed authorities of the accident. A police car and an ambulance were immediately dispatched to the scene. The boy was conscious upon arrival of the rescue crew but died en route to St. Joseph's Hospital.

"Mr. Gregg informed reporters that his son had been spending the night at the home of a friend in the Mountain Road area and evidently decided to return home during the evening. The bicycle did not have a light or reflectors.

"Police are looking for the car that struck young Gregg. Paint deposits on the bicycle show it to have been light blue in color.

"Daniel is survived by his parents...a half brother...a half sister...a maternal grandfather...two aunts...an uncle...."

Ray folded the article and put it back into the envelope. His own address stared up at him in the same black, hand-printed letters that had formed the message to Julie.

It's not a joke, he told himself. *It's not a joke at all.*

Not that he had ever really believed that it was. Since Julie had thought so, there had seemed little sense in pursuing the matter. It was possible. It might have been a joke. And she had managed to convince herself.

In his heart, even then, he had been pretty sure that it wasn't.

So it's caught up with us, he thought, *finally.* His own lack of surprise was the thing that surprised him. It was as though he had known all along, somewhere deep within himself, that this was going to happen. It was why he had come home, and a year ago it was why he had gone away.

The Raymond Bronson of a year ago had been a pretty spineless individual. He had always been small, which was part of it. It wasn't so much that he was short—five-foot-nine was a passable height—as the fact that he was lean and light-boned and not particularly well-muscled. In some families, this would not have mattered. When you were the only son of a man who had once been a professional football player, it mattered a lot.

Herb Bronson, Ray's father, had been known in his youth as The Booter. Friends from early days still called him that, and he sometimes referred to himself that way in a half-joking manner.

"Dinner ready yet?" he would call out as he came in the door in the evening. "The Booter's hungry enough to eat a bull!"

And Mrs. Bronson, busy in the kitchen, would laugh and call back, "How lucky for me! Braised bull is just what I'd planned to serve!"

The Booter had not had a particularly long or glorious career. He had received a knee injury in his second year as a defensive halfback and had reluctantly retired from professional athletics. He was, however, a highly successful businessman. Bronson's Sporting Goods Store had been the first of what eventually became a small chain of stores in two southwestern states.

Ray's build had been a disappointment to The Booter, and he had always known it. At the same time, he had known that his father loved him. Teasing comments were tempered with affection.

"Hey, Twerp," Herb Bronson would say jovially, "when are you going to put some weight on?" And at Christmastime, half the stock in the Bronson stores would appear beneath the tree: footballs, shoulder pads, bats and rackets, boxing gloves and camping gear.

Ray had not done badly in the minor sports; he was a member of the high school golf team and could play a decent game of tennis. It was football that was beyond him. He had managed to make the B Squad in junior high because a number of his contemporaries had not yet acquired their full growth, but suddenly, upon entering high school, he had found himself surrounded by towering individuals with weights up to and above two hundred pounds.

The boys were friendly and most of them knew The Booter by reputation. If he could not compete with them physically, Ray was superior to many of them academically. They respected him for this, and as he was a natural-born teacher, he often made himself useful in a tutoring capacity. No major athlete himself, he did have athletes for friends.

The first time he brought Barry Cox home with him for dinner, his father and Barry had sat over tall glasses of milk for two full hours after the meal was over, reviewing plays from Herb's career and more recent ones from Barry's experiences.

"That's a sharp kid," Mr. Bronson had remarked late that evening after Barry had left for home. "He's going to make it big, I'll bet. He's a good friend of yours, Twerp? You and he hang out a lot?"

"Yes," Ray had said.

"Good stuff," his father had commented approvingly. "I like to see you with friends like that." And later that year when he had started dating Julie James, there had been a similar reaction.

"Got a cheerleader for a girlfriend, huh? Chip off the old block, aren't you! Cuties of the school they were in my day. It took a real man to hook a cheerleader."

Julie had been more than that. Much more. But this he had not told his father. He had just crooked an eyebrow and made a little "here's to us" motion with his hand, and his father had clapped him on the shoulder in a man-to-man way. It was disappointing, sure, to have a son who couldn't make it in your footsteps, but Ray was there in spirit, doing his best, and The Booter knew it and respected him for it.

That was the Raymond Bronson of a year ago. Sometimes when Ray thought back upon himself, it was like looking at another person.

I wasn't anybody, he thought incredulously. *Not anyone real. I was kind of a shadow, partly Dad, partly Barry, not making it either way and not knowing how else I could make it. I don't know what Julie saw in me.*

But she had seen something.

"I love you," she had said once. Only once. They didn't get mushy very often. They usually just goofed around and had a good time.

But there had been one time when she had turned to him suddenly and had seen something in his face that had reflected back into hers. They hadn't even been making out or anything. It was right in the middle of a Sunday afternoon, and they had been sitting on the floor in the living room of the James' home playing some crazy card game, and out of the blue Julie had looked across at him and said, "I love you."

Well, that was in the past. She didn't love him now. That love had been snuffed out forever in one instant on one summer's night, as quickly and irrevocably as one little boy's life.

Barry had been driving too fast. Barry always drove too fast, when it came to that, but he drove well, and nobody got upset about it. Helen had been sitting close to him in the front seat. When he thought back, Ray could remember that, because he could remember her hair hanging over the back of the seat and swinging back and forth as the car took the curves.

Aside from that, he didn't remember much, because he had been making out with Julie most of the time during that ride. It was Ray's car, but as usual he and Barry had flipped for the back seat, and this time he had won. Julie had been sprawled in his arms, and she had been wearing a pink T-shirt that clung to her curves and slid up, revealing her flat stomach.

Suddenly, while they were kissing, Helen had screamed. The scream had brought them both upright in an instant. There had not been time to see much before it happened. The

46

bicycle had been there in front of them, caught in the glare of the headlights. They had seen the child from the back. He had been wearing a striped shirt. Then there was the thud and the crunch and then they were past.

"My god!" Julie had whispered from beside him. "We hit him!"

Ray had tried to answer, but somehow he could not get his voice working. The car had not stopped. It was moving on. It was going faster. It took the next curve with such speed that they were all thrown sideways, and Julie had fallen on top of him and had lain there, clutching him, whispering over and over, "Ray, Ray, we hit him."

"Go back!" Ray had managed to croak. "We've got to go back!"

"Go back?" Barry yelled over his shoulder. "What good would that do?"

In the seat beside him Helen was sobbing wildly.

Julie leaned forward, pulling away from Ray.

"That little boy! We've got to go back and help him!"

"Help him? We're not doctors. We couldn't do anything." Barry had slowed down a little now and was driving more evenly. "Once we get back into town we'll call for an ambulance. That's the best kind of help we can give him."

"We can't want until then," Ray said. "I'm calling now."

"Not yet," Barry told him. "Give it a couple of minutes till we're onto the freeway."

And, frozen in place, Ray had waited as Barry had

47

instructed—a wait he now realized was unforgiveable. It was ten whole minutes before he punched in 911.

"There's been an accident," he said frantically, "on Mountain Road, south of Silver Springs. It's just above the junction with 301. We hit a kid on a bicycle."

"Who is making this call?" the voice of the emergency operator asked.

"My name is—" Ray began.

"Don't say anything more," Barry shouted, and Ray, obeying on instinct, hit the "off" button.

"You told them enough," Barry continued more quietly. "You said what happened and where. There'll be an ambulance up there in a couple of minutes. There's no sense giving our names."

"They'll get them when we go back," Ray said. He paused, full realization beginning to sweep over him. "We are going back, aren't we?"

"For what?" Barry asked.

"Because! Because—we have to."

"We don't have to do anything," Barry said.

In the front seat, Helen had stopped sobbing. Julie said nothing. She seemed as zonked out as a zombie. There was not enough light to see either of their faces.

"Barry doesn't want to go back," Ray told them, since neither seemed to be taking in Barry's statement.

"I don't either," Helen said. "But I guess we have to, don't we? Oh god, I don't want to go back and see...see what we did." She drew in a strangled breath and began to cry again, very softly.

"It's not what we want to do," Julie said tonelessly. "It's what we have to do. It's the law."

"That sounds real noble." Barry pulled into the far left lane of the freeway, being very careful to keep just under the speed limit. "It's a great decision for you to make, but who do you think is going to get hit with a manslaughter charge if the kid up and dies? I was driving, not you. And I'm the only one here who no longer ranks as a juvenile."

"That's right," Ray said. "You're eighteen."

"Damned right, I am. No juvenile court for me. It's the real thing. I'll get tried as an adult."

"But it was an accident," protested Helen. "We all can testify to that. That bike came out of nowhere. We went around a curve and there it was. No lights. No reflectors. It wasn't our fault."

"Do you think that would make any difference?" Barry asked her. "The facts are that we've been out partying. We all had some beer and smoked pot tonight. The cops will spot that the moment we get out of the car. And it's a hit-and-run. Oh, sure, Ray called in a report. But technically it's a hit-and-run. About the worst charge you can get hit with."

"He might not be dead," Julie said. "He's probably only injured."

"Still, it's a hit-and-run."

"I'm responsible too," Ray said. "After all, it's my car."

49

"You would have been driving it too, if you hadn't won the toss." Barry turned to look back at him. "You're the bright guy who skipped a grade. You're still only seventeen. You want to turn yourself in, go back and do it."

"You mean, let them think I was driving?" Despite himself, Ray could not keep the horror from his voice.

"You could," Helen said. "If you're that determined to confess. The worst that could happen is that you might get your license taken away for a few months. It is your car, and like Barry says, it was just pure luck that you weren't the one driving it."

"That's ridiculous!" Julie spoke up sharply. "He wasn't driving and it would be stupid for him to say he was. It would be on his record forever."

"So it's all right for Barry to get a jail sentence, but heaven forbid that your Ray might get a splotch on his record?" Helen's voice was shaky with emotion. "What kind of friends are you to want to offer Barry up like some kind of human sacrifice? You don't have anything to lose. He does."

"She's got a point," Ray said quietly. "It would all be on Barry. He isn't any more responsible actually than the rest of us, except that he happened to be the one who was driving."

"Driving too fast," Julie said. "You know he was. He always drives too fast."

"Have you ever objected before?" Barry asked bitterly. "If you were all that concerned about my driving, why didn't you say so? You were awfully anxious to get into the back seat

50

tonight. 'Oh, Ray, Ray—we won! We won!' You knew I was a little bit high. It didn't bother you then."

"Let's take a vote," Helen said. "Let's decide that way."

There was a moment's silence. Then Barry said, "Okay. How about you two in the back, do you agree to stick by a vote?"

"It'll be two to two," Julie said.

"Then we'll flip."

"You don't flip about things like this."

"How else are we going to decide it?"

"We have to vote," Helen said. "It's the only thing we can do. I vote we don't go back. We just go home and let the police and doctors and people take care of things. What good would our going back there do? We couldn't help."

"I vote with Helen," Barry said.

"Well, I don't," Julie said adamantly. "I vote we go back...*now.*"

"Then you'll abide by the final vote?" Barry pressed her.

"By a vote, but not by a flip. If it's two to two, I'm holding out for going back." She turned confidently to Ray.

"I...I vote..." He looked at Barry. He could not see him well in the dark car, but he could see the tense way he was sitting, the way his hands were clenched on the steering wheel.

In the distance there came the wail of a siren.

"He's my best friend, Julie," Ray said softly.

She stared at him in disbelief.

51

"You don't mean you're voting with them? Ray, you can't be!"

"Like Barry says, what good would it do to go back now? The damage is done. He'll have all the help he needs, poor kid, before we could even get there. It would be so unfair, letting Barry take the blame for all of us."

"I don't believe it," Julie whispered. "I just don't believe you're really saying this."

There was a long silence. Then Barry said, "That's it, then. We've made a pact, and no one can break it. Now, let's get back into town and split up and go home."

The next morning it had been in the paper. Ray had read it at breakfast. Sitting there at the table, hearing his father's voice reading aloud from the sports page, smelling the plate of pancakes his mother had just placed before him, he had stared down at the story, on page two next to the obituaries, and he had known he was going to be sick.

"Daniel Gregg...conscious upon arrival of the rescue crew...died en route to St. Joseph's Hospital...."

"Excuse me," he had mumbled, getting quickly to his feet. "I-I'm not too hungry."

"Why, Ray!" his mother had exclaimed in concern, but he made it out of the room before she could stop him.

Later he called Julie. Mrs. James had answered the phone.

"Julie isn't feeling well this morning, Ray," she had told him. "Why don't you call back this evening?"

He had, and Julie had answered. Her voice had sounded small and thin.

"I don't want to talk," she had said. "Not now. Not about anything." And he had known then that it was over. He had placed the receiver back on the hook and lowered his face into his hands and, for the first time since he had been a little boy, he had cried.

Now, almost a full year later, he stood, staring again at the story, and the same cold feeling touched his heart. The clipping was yellowed from exposure. Someone had handled it often and read it many times. It was creased down the middle and had the smell of old dollar bills. Someone had kept it in a wallet, perhaps, drawing it out at odd times during the day to look at it, to dwell upon it. Someone had finally come to a decision and had addressed an envelope and mailed the clipping to an eighteen-year-old boy named Raymond Bronson.

Why? Ray asked himself. *Does the person who sent this really know something, or is he just guessing? What does he know, exactly, and who is he, and how does he know it? And most important of all—what is he going to do next?*

CHAPTER 6

On Memorial Day, Barry Cox had dinner with his parents. The conversation at the table was about the coming summer; his mother wanted him to spend it at home.

"Then in August," she said, "I thought we could take a little trip to the East Coast, just you and me. I know how you love to drive the Lexus, and it's been a good four years since we visited Aunt Ruth and Uncle Harry. If Dad can get away for a week, he could fly and meet us there. We might even take a few days in New York and see some shows."

"Mom, I don't know," Barry told her. "I've sort of got some other things in mind for the summer."

"You do?" Mrs. Cox looked surprised. "For heaven's sake, what?"

"Summer school?" his father asked. "A job?"

Mr. Cox was a quiet man, a number of years older than his wife. His hair was gray; Barry could not remember it ever having been any other color. He was an electrical engineer who worked for Sandia National Laboratories, and his mind and eyes often seemed to be focused on a spot a little beyond the reach of anyone else.

"Lou Wheeler and one of the other guys are taking off for Europe," said Barry. "They're going to spend the summer bumming around over there—hiking, sleeping in hostels— you know, the whole bit. They want to know if I'll go with them."

"That sounds like a pretty expensive three months," Mr. Cox commented dryly.

"Not really. College kids get some sort of reduced plane fare over, and the hostels are almost free. Food doesn't cost any more than it does here."

"It doesn't sound like a very nice way to see Europe." Mrs. Cox rested her salad fork on the side of her plate. "I had Europe in mind for you as a graduation present, a very special trip where we would stay in nice hotels and eat at famous restaurants, the ones you always read about, and go to concerts and, oh, everything. It was going to be a surprise."

"That's three years away," Barry said.

"They'll pass quickly, dear. Too quickly. It doesn't seem possible that you've almost completed a whole year of college." His mother smiled at him fondly. "You need a summer to relax and get to know your own family again. You've been so wrapped up in your studies lately that we've hardly even seen you."

It was the same old tune he'd heard a million times before. His teeth were on edge and his toes were boring holes in the bottoms of his shoes by the time he finally got back to the frat house.

When he entered his room, he found a card game in progress. A table had been hauled in from the living room and four guys were seated around it.

Lou Wheeler, his roommate, was dealing and paused long enough to greet him. "Hey, Cox, where've you been? Your Future Star's been trying to get hold of you."

"Oh?" Barry shoved the door closed and sat down on the edge of his bed. "I've been doing the duty call on the folks, trying to get them to come through with some bread for the summer. And my cell is dead."

The boy on Lou's right glanced up in surprise.

"I thought your old man was loaded."

"He is, but it's Mom who dispenses it. It was a nightmare to drive through the campus. They're having a fireworks display over at the stadium and there's a hell of a traffic jam."

"Some of the kids are going to stage an anti–Memorial Day demonstration — black banners, the works. Who needs a day to honor war?" Lou started to sort his hand. "Aren't you going to call Helen? She sounded pretty hot to see you."

"I'll call her in the morning," Barry told him.

Lou gave a whistle. "You nuts or something?" He gestured

toward the dresser. "Get a load of that picture! Can you guys imagine putting off a hottie like that?"

There was general laughter and a few crude but good-natured remarks from the other players. Helen's picture became the subject for general study.

"If you're tired of her," one boy said, "just pass along her phone number."

"I just might do that," said Barry.

He too glanced at the picture and continued studying it after the others had turned back to the game. It was Helen's junior class picture, the one she had submitted to the TV station, enhanced by Photoshop. The hair was a little too gold and the shade of the eyes was off. Across the bottom right corner Helen had written in her round, childish script, "With all my love, Heller."

It had meant something when she had given it to him, but now it had become just another item on the dresser. He seldom looked at it, but he had to admit that it made a nice showpiece.

Helen herself was a good showpiece, which was one reason he had not dropped her. He had never expected their relationship to continue on past high school. In fact, in the beginning, he had never anticipated it becoming a "relationship" at all.

He had been driving home from school and had seen her there, walking along the sidewalk, swinging her hips a little in that way she had. She was stacked. Even from the back he had been able to tell that. When he pulled up beside her, he had seen that she was even better from the front.

That first date had been a spur-of-the-moment decision. She was a looker, she was available, and he didn't have any other plans for the evening.

Then his mother had gotten into the act.

"A girl with a shape like that," she had said, "might at least wear a bra. And that hair color can't be natural. Nobody has hair that gold. Barry, dear, with all the really nice girls around—Ann Stanton, for instance, and the Webers' pretty little daughter—do you really want to spend your time and money on someone like this?"

That, of course, had cinched it.

"Sure," Barry had said. "I like her." Until that moment he had not really thought much about it. "She gets around," he had added, which had sent his mother into a spin. After that, he was publicly committed. Helen Rivers was his girl.

He had meant to wind the thing up before he started college. His original hope was that it would happen naturally when he left to attend an out-of-state school. That hadn't worked out. He had not been offered a football scholarship anywhere tempting, and his mother had decided that he should attend the local university.

"Then you'll be close," she had told him. "You can even live at home if you want to, and if you pledge a fraternity you can at least come home on the weekends."

So he had planned to make the break with Helen at the end of the summer.

Then two things had happened. First, there was that

damned accident. Helen had come to his defense then like a real trooper; he knew it was doubtful that Ray and Julie would have agreed to the pact if Helen hadn't been there pushing it. He owed her something for that, and he knew it, so he decided to postpone the breakup for a little while.

Then, out of the blue, came the Future Star bit. He had to admit that had impressed him, all the publicity and the glamour of having a girlfriend who was suddenly on television and known to everybody in town. It looked good to be seen around with the Channel Five Future Star hanging onto you. People were always pointing her out and coming up to ask if she was really Helen Rivers.

But enough was enough. The whole thing was getting far too clingy. A girl with looks like hers wasn't supposed to be insecure, but Helen seemed to be an exception. She was always asking for reassurance. "Do you like this outfit, Barry? Do you think my hair looks good this way? Does it look to you like I've put on weight since last summer?"

And even worse, she was beginning to talk about getting married. Married, and here he was, barely nineteen, and had never done anything, never been anywhere.

"No dice, Heller," he had told her. "I've got another three years of school before I can even think about it."

"That wouldn't matter," she kept insisting. "A lot of people get married while they're in college. I wouldn't mind working. In fact, I'd like it."

"Screw that. I wouldn't want a wife of mine working."

It was the first response he could think of, and even to his own ears the statement had sounded ridiculous. All married women worked, at least until they had babies. Would Helen expect to have children? Yes, probably she would. A screaming, puking infant as quickly as possible.

Shuddering, he had chided himself for his lack of guts.

He should simply have told her, "I've got a lot of living to do before I put down roots, and even when I do it's not going to be with you." Sometimes Helen reminded him of his mother, which was crazy because you could look through the world and never find two people with less in common. Still, when he was with them, he had the same feeling of near suffocation.

Ray Bronson had taken off for a year, ditched college and gone bumming up and down the coast of California, hardly keeping in touch with anybody. There had been times over the past months when the thought of Ray had filled Barry with a raging envy. Just the idea of being out from under his parents' rule with no pressure! And then the rational part of his mind would come to the fore; sure it sounded romantic, but who would really want to work at one crappy little job after another, waiting tables and washing cars and crewing on fishing boats, just to put food in your mouth and pay for a place to sleep?

The fact had to be faced, if you wanted your parents to pay the bills, you lived the way they wanted you to. But Helen, that was something else. He didn't have to stick it out with Helen. It had been a good thing for awhile, but when a good thing became a drag, it was time for it to end.

Out in the hall the telephone was ringing. After a few rings it stopped.

There was a knock on the door.

"Cox in there?" somebody called. "Phone call."

"Probably another female," Lou said with ill-concealed envy in his voice. "Man, what is it you've got? Will you sell me the formula?"

"Charm. Just charm."

Barry got up off the bed. As he passed the dresser he reached out and flipped the picture onto its face. Tomorrow he'd get rid of it and wipe the slate clean. Meanwhile, he'd get the hard part over with, and by phone was better than face-to-face. He had told Helen he'd call her, and he hadn't, so she'd be starting out the conversation with a chip on her shoulder. He could react to that, get mad at her for being unreasonable when she knew he was bogged down with studies. It wouldn't be a bad way to handle it.

Two of his frat brothers were coming down the hall as he reached the house phone.

"Make it a quick one, Cox," one of them said good-naturedly. "I've got a hot night to set up."

"I won't be long," Barry told him. "I can guarantee that. But there might be an explosion." The phone receiver was dangling at the end of the cord. He fished it up and clapped it to his ear.

"Cox here."

A few moments later he placed the receiver back on the hook and turned to the boys behind him. "It's all yours."

"Man," the first of the boys looked at him with a combination of admiration and amazement, "if I talked to my girl like that, she'd shoot me." He reached for the telephone and began to dial.

Barry walked down the hall and out the side door into the parking area. The sky in the west, over the stadium, was aglow with tiny red stars. They flew wide apart and faded and disappeared like drops of water on a hot griddle. A muffled cheer went up from the crowd that was watching the fireworks display.

Barry followed the sidewalk to its end, crossed the street and entered the athletic field. At the far end of it, the bleachers loomed, a dark mass against the sky. They were thrown into abrupt silhouette as another rocket went up at the stadium, and the audience burst into a roar of approval.

Barry stood still, trying to accustom his eyes to the sudden changes from light to dark. Then a flashlight suddenly went on right in front of him, the beam directed straight into his face.

"Hey, what the hell?" He raised his hands to protect his eyes.

There was enough noise from the fireworks so that he would not have known that the next sound was a gunshot, except he felt the bullet tear through his stomach and into his spine.

CHAPTER 7

They all learned about it that night.

Ray heard from his father. The Booter, who had been doing some paperwork in his den while listening to a ball game on the radio, went upstairs and rapped on his son's door.

"Ray?" he boomed. "A rotten thing has happened to a buddy of yours."

When Ray opened the door, his father told him about the news bulletin that had broken into the program, how Barry William Cox, nineteen, a University freshman, had been found by a campus patrolman, lying gravely wounded in the middle of the athletic field.

Students in the area were being questioned, but no one remembered hearing a shot.

"There was so much noise going on," one girl commented,

"that with all the holiday fireworks, one more bang would hardly have been noticed by anybody."

Another student, a fraternity brother of the Cox boy, reported having overheard a phone conversation only a short time before the shooting occurred.

"He was making arrangements to meet somebody," the student stated. "Knowing Barry, it was probably a girl. He was real short on the phone like he was pissed off about something."

According to the radio report, the injured man had been transported by ambulance to St. Joseph's Hospital.

Ray immediately called the hospital. He was told that Barry Cox was in surgery. No information about his condition was available.

His second call was to the home of Barry's parents. There was no answer. His third call was to Julie.

Helen Rivers learned about the shooting in a bizarre manner. She was standing in the television studio, waiting to deliver a weather report, filling in for the regular weatherman, who was sick. To her horror, she heard the newscaster, who was seated some six feet away from her, present the bulletin as part of the ten o'clock news.

Luckily, the camera was not on her face at the time.

A few moments later, to her own amazement, she calmly informed viewers that the high that day had been eighty-two, the low that night was expected to be sixty-eight, and there had been some rain in the northern part of the state.

Then, when the camera left her, she went into the ladies' room and descended into hysteria.

Collie Wilson was watching the news program on the big-screen TV in the common lounge of Four Seasons Apartments. When he heard the report of the shooting, he got into his car and drove to the television studio.

"I've come for Helen Rivers," he said to the first person he met after walking through the door.

"Thank god!" the man said. "We've got her lying down in the lounge. We didn't know what to do about her. She wants to go down to St. Joseph's."

"I'm here to take her," Collie said.

"Well, come on then. Just get her out of here."

The man led the way down a hall and through a door and down another hall. Collie could hear Helen long before he reached her.

When he came into the room he wondered for a moment if he had found the right person. The girl before him was a mess. Her eyes were red and swollen and her mascara had run down her cheeks in long black streaks. Her face was contorted with weeping.

"Hey," Collie said. "Remember me? Your friend by the pool?" He sat down beside her and put his hands on her shoulders. "Look, you'd better cut this out. It's not getting you anywhere. You want a ride to the hospital?"

Helen nodded, choking down the sobs.

65

"Then get ahold of yourself. Go wash your face or something. You can't go anywhere looking like this. I'll be waiting for you out in the lobby."

He went out into the front room, and a few moments later Helen came out to meet him. She had obeyed his command. Her face was clean and she had brushed her hair.

Collie took her arm and steered her out to the car and deposited her in the front seat. Then he went around to the driver's side and got in beside her.

"Why don't you turn on the radio?" he suggested. "There might be an update."

Obediently Helen reached over and pushed the button that controlled the radio. Immediately soft music filled the car. She started to turn the dial.

"Leave it where it is," Collie said. "That's the local news station. If there are going to be any reports, that's where we'll get them."

Helen sat back in the seat and spoke to him for the first time. Her voice was thin, like a lost child's.

"How did you know?"

"I was watching the Channel Five News. I do that a lot lately. A friend of mine on there gives the weather report sometimes."

"I can't believe it," Helen said. "Things like this just don't happen. Why would anybody shoot Barry?"

"You tell me," Collie said. "You know the guy. Is he the kind of person to have enemies?"

66

"Oh, no," Helen said promptly. "Barry's the best. Everybody adores him. He was voted most popular in our senior class in the yearbook. I'm the one the girls all hated because I was his girlfriend."

"Maybe it was robbery."

"At the college? College kids don't carry a lot of money around with them."

"Dope?"

"Barry doesn't do drugs. Oh, he smokes a little weed now and then, but nothing hard. You don't shoot somebody to get one joint." Her voice was shaking. "I love him, Collie. He loves me too. Someday we're going to get married. When he gets out of college, or even before! I don't mind working. . . ."

"Of course you don't."

"He thinks I'd mind. It's old-fashioned of him, isn't it? But nice. He thinks it wouldn't be right to marry somebody and have her work. He's just so marvelous! When I first met him, it was two years ago. He picked me up one day, when I was walking home from school. He said I was pretty."

"He was right," Collie said. At the moment the statement was not true, but this he discounted. He took his right hand from the wheel and reached over to give her an awkward pat on the shoulder.

"You hang on now, okay? Going to pieces like you did back there in the studio won't help anything. You don't seem like the kind of girl who falls apart in an emergency."

"I'm usually not," Helen said. "It's just that this is Barry."

67

"Well, hang in there. We'll be at the hospital in a few minutes, and then you'll know more about what happened. Whatever it is, you take it head on. Okay?"

Helen reached up to touch the hand on her shoulder.

"You'll come in with me, won't you?"

"Sure."

They drove the rest of the way in silence, except for the music, which stopped at last when Collie turned the key in the ignition to shut the engine off.

The hospital lobby was all but deserted. The gray-uniformed woman at the admitting desk sent them to the second floor, and a nurse there directed them down the hall to a small waiting room.

Several people were there already.

"Mrs. Cox!" Helen cried, breaking away from Collie's side to rush over to a thin-faced blond woman in a beige pantsuit.

The man next to her was portly and gray-haired with tired eyes. Automatically, as though from force of habit, he began to rise to his feet, and the woman put out a hand to gesture him down again.

"Hello, Helen," she said. "I'm surprised to see you here."

"Surprised!" Helen exclaimed. "How could I not be here! Oh, Mrs. Cox, I can't believe it! I just can't!"

Her eyes filled and she reached out as though to embrace the woman. Mrs. Cox drew back slightly and gestured toward the other people who were with them.

"Myrna, Bob, this is Helen Rivers, a classmate of Barry's

68

last year. These are the Crawfords, our dear friends and next-door neighbors."

"How do you do," Helen said dutifully. The stony faces of Barry's parents seemed to bewilder her. She turned to Collie. "This is Collingsworth Wilson. He's a friend. He lives in the same apartment complex."

"Barry has lots of friends," Mrs. Cox said. "I'm glad to see that most of them had the good taste not to come trooping down here. This isn't a circus, Helen. There's nothing to see. It's my boy in there—*my* boy—terribly hurt! Maybe dying!"

Abruptly she raised her hands and covered her face. The rings on her fingers twinkled under the overhead light. Watching her, Collie found himself wondering how she ever managed to use her hands, as encumbered as they were.

Mr. Cox put an arm around his wife's shoulders.

"Now, Celia," he said gruffly. "Chin up, dear." He turned to Helen. "You'll have to forgive her. She's very upset. We all are. It was thoughtful for you and your friend to come down here, but I do think it might be better if we kept it to close friends and family. Right at this point anyway."

Helen's face was white.

"She said he might be dying!"

"He has the best care, the best doctors."

"What are they doing to him in there?"

"Send her away," Mrs. Cox cried. "My god, how much of this do we have to be put through? If she hadn't phoned him, if she hadn't insisted on dragging him out to meet her, this wouldn't have happened."

"What do you mean?" Helen asked. She turned to Mr. Cox. "What is she talking about?"

"We're not blaming you, Helen," Barry's father said. "We know the last thing on your mind was bringing harm to Barry. Nevertheless, it was your phone call that brought him out onto the playing field in the dark. Of course, you were not directly responsible for this tragedy, but if you had left him alone, let him stay in the frat house and study, which is what he should have been doing—"

"But I didn't talk to him tonight," Helen said in confusion. "I called him once early this evening. I wanted to tell him something somebody had done, a thing on my door...." She brought herself under control with an effort. "He was supposed to call me this weekend. He promised. And when he didn't...I had to tell him. But he wasn't there. I called about five, and he was out, and I left word for him to call me back, but he didn't."

"We're set for a long wait here, dear." Mrs. Crawford spoke up quietly and her voice was not unkind. "The Coxes have your number, I'm sure. We'll see that you are called when there is something definite to report. In the meanwhile, I think you'd better go. I really do."

"But, Barry and I—I'm not just a school friend. I'm more, a lot more—" Helen's voice was rising sharply.

"Come on," Collie said softly. "I think we'd better go somewhere else to wait. People here are upset enough. Okay?"

"But," Helen began, "I don't understand."

Gently he took her arm and turned her around. "Come on."

Nobody spoke to call them back. Still holding her arm, he steered her down the hall to the elevator.

"There are other waiting rooms. We'll sit in the lobby. We'll have that whole place to ourselves. You can yell or cry or anything you want, and it won't bother anybody."

"I don't want to yell," Helen said. "I want to wait here, outside of surgery. This is where the news will come when there is any. I'm not just anybody, Collie. I'm Barry's girlfriend! I'm the one he's going to marry someday!"

"Maybe so," Collie said, "but his mother doesn't seem to be in on the secret." He pressed the button for the elevator, and as they rode down he did not loosen his hold on her arm.

Julie James placed the receiver back on the hook and went into the living room.

"Mom," she said. "Somebody's shot Barry Cox."

Mrs. James, who was kneeling on the floor, cutting around a dress pattern, straightened up with a gasp. "Why, Julie, how awful! Barry Cox? The boy who goes out with Helen?"

"That was Ray on the phone," Julie told her. "He heard it on the radio. No, I guess he said it was his dad who heard it. It happened over at the U, on the athletic field. They don't know who did it."

Her voice was flat and emotionless with shock.

"I was afraid there might be some trouble over there

tonight," Mrs. James said. "That Memorial Day fireworks display should never have been held on campus, not with student unrest the way it is today. The six o'clock news mentioned the fact that some of the students were gathering for a demonstration. But for them to have taken it this far—to have had one of your friends injured—why, it's just incredible! Is he badly hurt?"

"Ray didn't know. He called the hospital, and they wouldn't tell him anything." Julie dropped to her knees beside her mother.

The dress on the floor was to be for her. It was pink. The bright material swam before her eyes.

"Do you think it was the war demonstration?" she asked. "Do you really think it was that? Could somebody have had a gun at the demonstration?"

"What other answer could there be?" her mother asked her.

CHAPTER 8

Helen awoke to the sound of a motor running. The waking was gradual; at first the sound was there at the back of her consciousness as part of a dream, and then it seemed to grow louder and louder so that the dream itself was lost in the roar. Then she became aware of the fact that she was in bed and that the sound was not within her head at all but from someplace outside of herself.

She opened her eyes to find the room flooded with morning sunlight. Below her bedroom window the Four Seasons caretaker was cutting the grass with a power mower.

I slept, Helen thought in amazement. *How could I have slept so hard when Barry—*

Just the thought of his name brought her to a sitting

position. The happy-face alarm clock on the bedside table showed ten fifteen.

The morning's half over, Helen thought incredulously. *I've been asleep for over six hours!*

It had been three in the morning when Barry had been moved from surgery to the recovery room and the Coxes and their friends had stepped from the elevator into the lobby. Helen, who had been seated in a chair opposite the elevator door, had sprung to her feet.

"What? How?"

"They got the bullet," Mr. Cox told her wearily. "It was lodged in the spine. How much damage it did, they can't tell yet."

"But he's going to live?"

"Prognosis is good. He came through the surgery well. He's a strong boy; the doctor seems to think he's going to make it all right."

"Oh, thank god!" Weak with relief, Helen put out a hand to steady herself against the back of the chair. "I've been praying. I haven't stopped praying since I heard the news at the TV studio."

"Thank you," Mr. Cox said. "We're grateful for your concern."

Mrs. Cox and the Crawfords had crossed to the far side of the lobby. Mrs. Cox's face was white and drawn, and for the first time since she had met her, Helen thought the woman looked older than her husband.

74

"You're going home now?" Helen asked.

"Yes. My wife is exhausted. The doctor says there is no reason to remain here; it will be hours before Barry's anesthetic wears off and a good deal longer than that before he can have visitors. He suggests that we try to get some sleep, and that should apply to you too." He turned to Collie, who had risen to stand at Helen's side. "You'll see she gets home, Mr. Wilson?"

"Of course," Collie said. "I brought her down here."

"I won't be able to sleep," Helen said. "I don't think I'll ever sleep again."

But she had. The golden light of midmorning proved that. She had slept so hard that her body ached from having been so long in one position, and when she got out of bed her legs felt rubbery, as though they might give way at any moment.

She went out to the telephone in the living room and dialed the number of the hospital. The voice that answered told her that Barry Cox was "resting comfortably." He had been removed from the recovery room and was now in room 414-B. For the time being he was to be allowed no visitors except for family.

"But I'm sure he will want to see me," Helen insisted. "You'll ask him, won't you? Tell him it's Helen."

"Are you a member of the immediate family?"

"Not exactly."

"What is your relationship to the patient?"

"I'm a-a friend," Helen said. "A very good friend."

75

"The orders are that Mr. Cox is to have no visitors outside of the immediate family."

"Oh, damn," Helen muttered as she replaced the receiver. "I can imagine who made that rule—dear Mama Cox herself."

The events of the night before rose in her mind with the odd, unfocused quality of a nightmare: the announcement at the television station, Collie's arrival, the drive to the hospital, the cold, sharp hatred in the eyes of Barry's mother.

"If she hadn't phoned him," she had cried. "If she hadn't insisted on dragging him out to meet her—"

"But I didn't!" Helen had told her. "I didn't!"

They had not heard her, or they had heard but not listened.

"We're not blaming you, Helen," Mr. Cox had said, but in fact they were blaming her, both of them. Even though Mr. Cox had stopped to speak to her in the lobby, she had seen the blame in his eyes.

"I didn't," Helen said aloud now, her voice coming strange in the empty apartment. "I didn't call Barry to meet me out on the playing field. I didn't talk to him at all last night."

But there had been a phone call. A statement from one of Barry's fraternity brothers had confirmed that. Someone had called and talked to Barry and set up an appointment, someone whose request had seemed important enough to draw him out of the house in immediate response.

Who was it who had called and why? Was it a girl? Could Barry have another girl, someone he was seeing when he wasn't with her?

76

"No," Helen answered herself firmly. "No, of course not." She was Barry's girlfriend, his only girlfriend. If she couldn't trust Barry, then who on earth could she trust? And yet there had been things over the past year, odd, assorted little things, none too important in themselves, yet added together, enough to be slightly disturbing to someone less sure of his love than Helen.

There was that conversation with Elsa the night of the accident. Helen always thought of it that way, as "the accident," unpreventable, arranged somehow by the hand of fate. One moment they had been riding along, relaxed and happy, her head on Barry's shoulder, the car radio wrapping them in soft music, and the next moment the child had been there in front of the car. There was nothing Barry could have done about it. There had been no time for him to get his right arm back from around her and his right hand onto the steering wheel. Even if both hands had been on the wheel in the first place, it was doubtful that he could have swerved in time. They had done the best they could. Ray had called 911. It was not Barry's fault that the boy had been injured beyond help; no child of ten had any business riding his bicycle on a mountain road in the middle of the night.

It was not Barry's fault, it was none of their faults. Still, it had been a terrifying and dreadfully upsetting experience. She had cried a lot on the way home, and when she had come into the house, softly so as not to disturb her parents, she had not been prepared to find Elsa still awake with the light on, reading.

Elsa had glanced up from her movie magazine, and her eyes had narrowed behind her glasses.

"You've been crying!"

"No, I haven't," Helen had said.

"You sure have; your eyes are red as beets!" Elsa had laid aside the magazine with an air of somebody close to triumph. "What did he do, break up with you? I've been wondering how long it would take for him to get around to it."

"Don't be silly," Helen said. "Everything's just fine between Barry and me."

"Then why have you been crying?"

"I told you, I haven't been. It was just smoke in the car." Helen went to her side of the dresser and took her nightshirt out of the top drawer. She could feel Elsa's eyes focused on her back.

After a moment Elsa said, "If it didn't happen tonight, it will soon, you know."

"I don't know what you mean."

"You don't think Barry's going to stick with you now, do you? He's starting college in a couple of months."

"I don't know what difference that should make," Helen said, turning to face her sister. "He's going to the University, right here in town. He can see me every night if he wants to."

"But why should he want to?" Elsa asked her. "Face it, Helen, Barry's a catch for somebody. He's good-looking, his family has money, he's a big football hero—every girl's dream guy. There are a lot of sexy girls going to the University, real

78

women with brains and background. How do you think you're going to stack up?"

"Barry loves me," Helen said defensively.

"Has he ever told you that?"

"Well, not in those words exactly. But there were plenty of other girls in high school too. I'm the one he picked."

"High school's different," Elsa said. "Guys look for different things then, kid things. Big boobs and highlights in your hair, that's cool stuff in high school. College guys are different. They're looking for quality."

"You're cruel," Helen said softly. She stood, staring down at her sister's heavy, doughish face, at the pursed little mouth already indented at the corners with grooves of discontent. "You're just jealous. Boys don't like you, they never have. You never had anybody like Barry. You're jealous because I do."

"I'm not jealous of you. I'm sorry for you."

"That's a lie," Helen said. "Barry's not going to drop me. I may not have a high society background and folks with money and things like that, but I've got a lot to offer that other girls don't."

Elsa regarded her coolly. "Like what, for instance?"

"Like...like..." Helen floundered for words.

"Dream on," Elsa said and picked up her magazine. "You just keep dreaming on."

The next day Helen had taken her junior class picture, a good picture that showed her fine bones and shining hair and bright, perfect smile, and entered it in the Channel Five Future

79

Star Contest. It turned out to be the smartest move she had ever made.

There was a rap at the door. Helen snapped out of her reverie with a jolt.

"Who is it?"

"Collie. Just checking to see how you got through the night."

"Wait a minute, will you? I'm just getting up." Hurriedly, Helen went to the bedroom and got a robe out of the closet. A glance in the mirror as she passed it caused her to stop to comb her hair and apply some lipstick. Collie might be no more than a platonic friend, but he was, after all, a male friend.

That fact was reflected in his eyes when she opened the door to him.

"I was going to ask you if you slept," he said. "I thought you'd be all haggard and baggy-eyed. I thought wrong."

"I did sleep," Helen told him with a touch of apology in her voice. "I don't know how I could, but I did. I was just going to make some coffee. Would you like some?"

"I already had some, thanks. I'm on my way out to my folks' place. Did you have a chance yet to call the hospital?"

"Barry's out of recovery and into a private room. They say he's 'resting comfortably,' whatever that means."

"I guess it means just that." He hooked his thumbs into his pants pockets. "I guess you'll be going over there after your webcast?"

"They're not permitting visitors."

"Then he's still on the critical list?"

"I don't know," said Helen, suddenly unaccountably irritated. "I don't know anything. Nobody tells me anything. I'd call the Coxes, but I'm sure Mrs. Cox would be the one to answer, and I bet she'd hang up on me."

"Don't blame her too much," Collie said. "She wasn't all there last night. Women get like that when something happens to a kid. My own mom's that way."

"Well, I was upset too," Helen reminded him. "I'll bet I was as upset as she was. They're letting the family see him. I'm tempted to go down there and pass myself off as his sister."

"No chance. Anybody who owns a TV will know who you are before you open your mouth." He was frowning a little. "Look, Helen, there's something I want to ask you."

"Yes?"

"Last night on the way over to the hospital, you told me Barry was a guy who didn't have any enemies. We ruled out a couple of other things too — robbery, dope. It kind of leaves us with nothing, doesn't it? I mean, no reason for the shooting at all?"

"I don't even want to think about it," Helen said shortly.

"But you need to think about it. You know Barry better than anybody. If he was mixed up in something shady, something illegal like selling pills or —"

"He wasn't. There's not even a question in my mind."

"I'm not saying it had to be that. It was just the first possibility that came into my head. Maybe it was something entirely different, but people don't usually get shot for nothing. Oh, once in awhile a gun goes off while somebody's cleaning it or a hunter fires at a deer and finds out it's another hunter, but something like this, where a guy gets lured out of the house by a phone call—well, it's planned. It has to have been."

"I don't believe that," said Helen.

"What do you believe, then? Do you have an answer? All I'm getting at is that you're the one who has the best chance of coming up with an answer, at least until Barry's able to talk himself."

"I can't think of anything."

"Okay, okay." He reached out and gave her chin a tap. "Keep it up. Enjoy your coffee. I'll see you later."

He was off down the hall, and Helen pushed the door shut behind him. It clicked into place and she turned to walk away from it. Then, slowly, she turned back and slid the bolt.

She went back into the bedroom. The sound of the lawn mower was dimmer now; the caretaker had moved over to a lawn across the way. The sunlight had shifted slightly, and shafts of gold fell across the rumpled bed and reached over to touch the alarm clock. On the dresser Barry's picture reigned supreme, surrounded by a jar of moisturizer, a compact of blush, a palette of eye shadow.

Helen crossed the room and opened the top drawer of the dresser. For a moment she stood there, as though afraid to reach inside. Then she did, and with an unsteady hand drew forth the magazine picture of the little boy on the bicycle.

CHAPTER 9

When school let out that afternoon Julie found Ray waiting for her. He was parked in the same spot where he used to park the year before when he was a student himself, over on the far side of the lot, away from the building.

She was not surprised to see him. Somehow she had expected to find him there. When she came through the door, she broke away from the stream of laughing, shoving students and turned automatically toward that spot. She crossed to the car and opened the door, just as she had done so many times in the year that was past, and tossed her books inside and climbed in beside them.

"It seems funny," she said by way of greeting, "to have you driving your dad's car."

"He's been pretty great about letting me use it," Ray said.

"I drive him down to the store in the morning, and Mom picks him up at night. It's odd, too, because he was plenty burned up about my taking off like I did last fall. He couldn't understand why I'd blow off school and go out on my own, and of course, I couldn't do any decent job of explaining."

"What did you do with your own car?" Julie asked him. "I never knew."

"Barry and I hammered the dent out and took it over to Hobbs and sold it to a farmer. I took a loss, but it was worth it to be rid of it." He started the engine. "Where do you want to go?"

"Anywhere. It doesn't matter."

"Up by the picnic place?"

"No. Not there." She answered so quickly that the three words came out as one. "How about going to Henry's? We could get a snack."

"You're hungry?"

"No, but we've got to go someplace. That's as good as anywhere else."

It wasn't, as they discovered after they got there. Henry's Ice Cream Shop was having a special on hot fudge sundaes, two for the price of one, and the news had traveled quickly. The lot was almost completely filled. Car horns honked and tooted, and there was a huge line at the window. Some of the junior high kids were climbing in and out of car windows and sitting on the hoods and shouting back and forth, while older high school students in other cars were yelling at them to be quiet.

"The picnic place?" Ray asked again.

Julie nodded, defeated. "I guess we don't have much choice."

They drove in silence up the curving road, and when they passed one particular spot, Julie shut her eyes and bit down hard on her lower lip. They continued to climb until they reached the sign that said "Cibola National Forest—Silver Springs." Then Ray turned the car down a narrow dirt road that led off to the left, away from the cleared area with the tables and benches. Branches brushed against both sides of the car, and a squirrel ran across the road in front of them as they came to the stream and pulled to a stop near the bank.

It was a few moments before either of them spoke.

Finally Ray said, "It's still the same."

Julie nodded. The thin, silver cord of water wound its way down from the rocks above them and disappeared below in a clump of evergreens. A scattering of nameless yellow flowers poked their heads from the fresh, spring earth, and beyond the trees the sky arched in a high, rich curve of blue.

"There was a sliver of moon caught in the branches of that pine tree," Ray said. "Remember?"

"I don't want to remember. Not anything about that night."

"Julie, you have to." He reached over to cover her hand with his. "We've got to remember—to think—to decide together what to do."

"Why?" Julie asked. "It's been over for almost a year now."

"No, it hasn't. Not really."

"What do you mean?"

"You can't just shove something like this under a rug and pretend it never has been. Especially now, after what's happened to Barry."

Julie drew her hand out from under his and folded it with her other hand in her lap. "What happened to Barry doesn't have anything to do with the other. He was shot during a student demonstration."

"No, he wasn't. There wasn't any shooting during the demonstration last night."

"Mom thinks—" she began.

"Face it, Julie, that demonstration was peaceful. A bunch of kids carrying signs, that's all it was. They sat in the road awhile, and the people who came to watch the fireworks had a hard time getting their cars out. There wasn't any violence. Nobody even fired off a cherry bomb."

"Let's drop it, shall we? I really don't feel like rehashing things."

"Julie, stop it!" Ray said sternly. "We've got to talk!"

"Oh, all right." She turned her face to his, and the pain in her eyes was so deep that he was momentarily sorry that he had forced the issue. "All right," she continued, "if you insist on talking about that night, then, yes, there was a moon in that pine tree. Yes, it was a beautiful picnic. Yes, we killed a little boy. Is there anything more?"

"There's Barry."

Julie sat quiet a moment, digesting the statement. Then she said slowly, "You think Barry was shot deliberately by somebody who knew what happened?"

"By the same person who wrote you that note and sent me the clipping."

"What clipping?" Julie asked. "I didn't know anything about a clipping."

"I got it Saturday. It came in the mail, just the way that note did to you. It was addressed in the same block printing."

Ray reached in his pocket and pulled out his wallet. He opened it and took out the folded newspaper column and handed it to Julie.

She took one glance and handed it back to him. "I don't have to read it, Ray. I remember it. I can quote it word for word."

"And what about Helen? Has she received anything in the mail?"

"Not in the mail," Julie said in a small voice. "There was something though. I talked to her Sunday. She thought Barry might have done it, that he was playing a trick on her."

"What was it?"

"A magazine picture," Julie said. "It was taped to her door. It happened on Saturday. According to Helen, she was sitting out by the pool and this new guy who has the apartment two doors down from her came out and pulled up a chair beside her. They sat and talked for awhile, and then

Helen got worried that she might be getting sunburned and went inside. When she got up to her apartment she found that somebody had taped a picture of a boy on a bicycle to her door. She said she thought maybe Barry had dropped over—he had said he'd be seeing her during the weekend—and had seen her there with another guy and thought he'd teach her a lesson."

"That doesn't sound like Barry," Ray commented. "He plays around enough himself so he wouldn't have any right to get jealous over Helen."

"But Helen doesn't know that. She doesn't go out with other people. Besides, not having the right to be jealous doesn't mean that a person doesn't get that way." Julie paused. "I'll admit it does sound pretty unlikely, but that's what Helen thought. She told me that if Barry didn't call her by noon on Monday she was going to phone him and have it out."

"Do you suppose that was what drew him out onto the athletic field?" Ray asked thoughtfully. "A phone call from Helen?"

"It could have been. The morning paper said he received a call from somebody right before he left the fraternity house."

"And then he was shot...."

"You don't think it was Helen!" Julie regarded him with horror. "That's ridiculous! Helen worships the very ground Barry walks on."

"Of course I don't think Helen shot him," Ray said. "She

wouldn't pick up a gun, much less pull a trigger, and she's crazy about Barry. I'm just thinking out loud, trying to look at it from all sides."

"If it wasn't Helen's phone call," Julie said, "somebody else must have known about it. Like you said, Barry isn't exactly the most faithful boyfriend a girl ever had. Who knows what might have been going on in other situations? There could have been girls he was seeing from the University who had jealous boy-friends— we can't know. And then there's the possibility of it being a totally unconnected accident, just some freak on a bad trip out walking around with a gun and not even knowing or caring who might get hurt. You read about things like that happening."

"It's possible," Ray admitted. "But it would be a strange coincidence after the things the three of us have received. Barry was the one who was driving that night."

"And he's the only one who didn't receive any memento of the accident. At least, as far as we know, he didn't."

"He received a bullet," Ray said.

The words hung there between them, stark in the soft spring sunshine.

Julie shuddered. "All right," she said quietly, "since you insist on saying it, let's suppose for a moment that the person who shot Barry is the same person who has been sending us the notes and pictures and clippings. It's the person who knows — or thinks he knows — about the accident. Then why has he waited so long? And why would he do something like this when all he

89

has to do, all he ever had to do right from the beginning, was report us to the police?"

"The part about waiting I can't answer." Ray shook his head. "About the other, well, he'd have to hate us. Hate us so much that he wants to kill us himself rather than let the authorities punish us in some other way."

"Who could hate like that?" Julie asked shakily.

"Whoever was closest to the kid, I guess."

"His parents?"

"That figures. I know how my folks would feel, or your mom. But then again we've got the question of the waiting. If the parents had been able to find out somehow—and I still can't see how they could have—why would they have waited almost a year to do something about it?"

"And how would they have known about Helen's phone call? If it *was* Helen's phone call. We don't even know that for sure."

"That's the one thing we can find out without any trouble," Ray said. "All we have to do is ask her. And as soon as they start allowing Barry to have visitors, we can find out a whole lot more. He might even have seen the person who shot him."

"At night? On a dark field?"

"The person saw him, didn't he? There must have been enough light to make it possible to aim a gun."

"Helen's still at the studio," Julie said, glancing at her watch. "She usually gets home around five. Let's go over there then and see what she has to tell us."

"That's fine with me," Ray said. "We can kill half an hour here until it's time for her to be home. Let's get out and walk along the bank like we used to. I've thought about this place so often during the past year. That sounds crazy, I guess. I mean, there I was with all that California sunshine and salt-water and white beaches, and I'd keep remembering what it was like here with the pine smell and the stream and-and . . . my own girl with me."

He had pushed it too far, and he knew it. He could see Julie stiffen.

"No," she said. "Look, give me that clipping."

"The thing about the accident?" He had put it back in his wallet. Now he got it out again, slowly, letting the wallet hang open an extra minute so that Julie could see her own picture smiling out at them. It was a year-old picture. She was wearing jeans and a tank top. Her hair hung loose and bouncy, and her eyes were crinkled up with laughter.

Now, as he handed her the clipping, Ray realized with a start how much her eyes had changed since that picture was taken. There was no hint of laughter in them now. They were eyes that had not laughed in a long time.

Julie took the article, careful not to brush Ray's hand with hers, and smoothed it flat.

". . . son of Michael and Mary Gregg," she read aloud, "of 1278 Morningside Road Northeast. That's near here, Ray. It's one of those little roads just south of the spot where we had the accident."

"I guess it is if the boy was riding home from a friend's house."

"Ray." She drew a long breath. "I want to go there."

"Where?"

"To his house."

"Are you crazy?" Ray asked incredulously. "What would you want to do a sick thing like that for?"

"It's no sicker than it was to come up here. You're the one who keeps saying that we've got to face it and relive it and figure out what it is that's happening. If we're going to do that, I think we ought to see his house and talk with his parents."

"Talk with his parents!" Ray was sure he was not hearing her correctly. "You mean we should just go up and ring the doorbell and say, 'We're two of the people who were in the car that ran down your son and we want to interview you and see how you feel about it?' You're out of your mind!"

"You know I don't mean that," Julie said sharply. "And I'm not out of my mind at all. We've agreed that the people who have the most right to hate us are the boy's mother and father. How are we ever going to find out about them if we don't see them?"

"You said 'talk with them.'"

"Yes, talk, but not about this. I thought—oh, Ray, couldn't we go up to the door and introduce ourselves and say we were having car trouble? We could tell them our cells died, and ask to use the phone. If they aren't the ones, they would never know

92

the difference. They'd just think we were a couple of teenagers who had been up here parking and couldn't get down again."

"And if they are the ones who are after us?"

"We'd know it," Julie said. "At least, I'm sure I would. When they saw us, when they heard our names, it would show on their faces. The shock of seeing us appear like that on their doorstep—"

"Could send them straight for their gun." Ray completed the sentence for her. "If they are the people who shot Barry, don't you imagine they'd like to add two more to the list?"

"In their own front yard?" Julie shook her head. "Be reasonable. It's broad daylight, and there are sure to be neighbors. It's different from the situation with Barry. Besides, I just can't believe someone's out to kill us all. I still think it's a drug freak, and that poor Barry happened into the wrong place at the wrong time, just like, well, like little Daniel Gregg did."

"I don't like it," Ray said. "Like I said, it's sick. I sure don't want to see them."

"But I do." Julie's voice was low and firm. It was the same voice that had stated so flatly a year ago, "It's over, Ray. Whatever it was that we had, it's over. I'm breaking free of you, of the others, of everything that will ever remind me of that awful night." She had meant that, and she meant this now.

"I want to see them," Julie said determinedly. "If we're facing this, then let's really face it. Let's know. I'm going to the house, and if you want to take me there, fine. If you don't, I'll take Mom's car and drive up there myself."

93

CHAPTER 10

The house was one of a cluster of little homes almost at the end of the narrow, unpaved road which led off to the east from the Mountain Highway. All the houses there were of masonry construction, small and white with pitched roofs, half lost in the shadow of the mountain, and set close to the road as though happy for this slim connection with civilization.

They passed it once to check the house number. Then they drove slowly back again and parked down the road, got out, and began the walk back.

With every step, Julie felt her heart contracting. When they finally came opposite the house again, she had reached the point of feeling physically ill.

Ray reached out and touched her arm.

"Are you sure you want to go through with this?"

"I'm sure," Julie said firmly.

Actually, she was no longer sure at all. The plan that had seemed so reasonable such a short time ago, now suddenly seemed ridiculous. What if, as Ray suggested, the Greggs actually were the people who had shot Barry and had mailed the insinuating notes and clippings? What if they did recognize the two people named Julie James and Raymond Bronson? What if their desire for revenge was so great that they didn't care about the consequences and did something violent?

Or, in a way almost as bad, what if they simply stood there in the doorway, shoulder to shoulder, with tears running down their faces, and asked, "Why? Why did you run down our son and never even come back to say you were sorry?"

This is his house, Julie thought, staring at it. *This is where Daniel Gregg lived.*

It was an ordinary enough house, and the front yard had a bedraggled, uncared-for look. The stubble of grass, not yet green with summer, grew in patches with the earth showing hard and bare in between, and the flower beds under the windows still held brown stalks from last year's garden. Along one side of the roof the faded trim showed a bright yellow, and a ladder leaned against the wall as evidence that someone was in the process of repainting.

"Come on," Ray said, "if you're coming." The words were impatient, but the voice that spoke them was merely nervous.

"I'm coming," she said, and hurried to catch up with him.

They mounted the cement step, and Ray placed his finger

hard on the doorbell. The door stood half-open, and through the screen they could see the simple furnishings of a living room: a green chair, the end of an over-stuffed couch, a coffee table holding magazines. Across the room an old portable TV set stood on a stand.

Despite the fact of the open door, the place held the feeling of emptiness.

Ray pressed the bell again, and they listened together as the sound rang through the house.

"No answer." He sounded relieved. "Nobody's home."

"Somebody has to be here," Julie insisted. "People don't just go off and leave their houses open like this."

"Mr. Gregg is probably at work. We didn't think about that. And maybe his wife works too or went next door."

"Are you looking for me?" The voice, coming from directly behind them, caused them both to jump as though caught in some guilty enterprise. They turned simultaneously and found themselves gazing down at a short, plump, pretty girl no more than a few years older than Julie.

"I was around at the side of the house, taking down the wash. Our dryer's conked out so we're back to the old-fashioned clothesline. I thought I heard the bell but I wasn't sure. Can I help you with something?"

"We were hoping to use your phone," Julie said, and Ray began at the same time. "Our car, we've had some trouble with it. It's back up the road a ways."

"Come on in." The girl joined them on the step and opened

the door, motioning them inside ahead of her. "Don't worry about the screen; there aren't any flies yet, thank the Lord. During the summer we have to keep the door closed every minute or they swarm all over us. The phone's right around the corner there in the hall, and there's a directory hanging over to the side on a nail. Do you see it?"

"Yes," Ray said, going into the hallway. "Thanks."

"If Pa was here he could probably get the car started for you. He's great with motors. I don't know a carburetor from a battery myself, but then I guess most girls don't, do they?" She smiled at Julie. It was a wide, sweet smile that lit up her face in such a familiar way that Julie found herself staring.

"Do I know you?" Julie asked. "I know this sounds silly, but I could swear I've seen you someplace."

"Maybe you have," the girl said easily. "I'm a hairdresser at the Bon Marche on Central. It seems like I've done the hair of half the people in town at one time or the other. My name's Megan."

"I'm Julie James," Julie told her, "and my friend is Ray Bronson. It's nice of you to help us like this."

The girl's smile didn't change. Nothing altered in the expression in the wide, dark eyes.

"Oh, I'm glad to have people drop by. Ma always says I can talk the ears off a rabbit, which is probably why I like beauty work. You get to talk to people all day long. But today was my regular day off, and we didn't work yesterday because of it's being a holiday, and then the day before that was a

Sunday, and with my folks out of town, I've been ready to climb the walls. Would you like some iced tea? You'll probably have a while to wait before somebody can get here to fool with the car. We're pretty far out."

"Tea would taste good," Julie said. "Thank you."

She followed the girl from the living room into the small, bright kitchen. The walls were a paler shade of yellow than the newly painted trim outside, and there was a calendar with a picture of kittens on it hanging under a clock. A magazine on the kitchen table lay open to a page of advertisements as though the recent reader had been trying to while away the empty hours. Megan opened the refrigerator and took out a plastic container of tea and poured it into three tall glasses.

"Do you want sugar?" she asked. "Or do you think your friend will?"

"No, thanks, I don't think so." Julie took the glass from the girl's small, square hand.

There's one thing for sure, she thought. *This girl isn't involved in this thing in any way. She certainly couldn't have anything to do with the attack on Barry and she doesn't recognize our names. She's as open and friendly as she can be.*

Megan picked up the remaining two glasses.

"Let's carry these outside while I finish taking down the wash. That's one thing about being the only one at home now, with my folks gone and my big brother out of the nest. There's nobody else to do the laundry and cooking and stuff.

I keep telling myself that I'm going to lose weight this way. I just hate to cook for myself, don't you? But it doesn't really work out like that. The foods with the most calories are the easiest things to fix."

"Where are your parents?" Julie asked as she followed Megan out the kitchen door into the backyard. It was a pleasant yard with a redwood picnic table and a charcoal grill and beyond that a tool shed, with a shaggy growth of trees enclosing it all.

To the left, on a clothesline stretched between two trees, blouses and slacks and a couple of bed sheets waved in the slight breeze.

"They're in Las Lunas," Megan said, setting the glasses down on the picnic table and crossing over to the line. "Ma's not well. She's in a hospital down there, and Pa moved down to be near her. He's staying in a boarding house so he can see her every day. The doctors say that's a good thing for her."

"What a shame!" Julie went over to stand beside her. "Here, let me help you fold that sheet. Has your mother been ill for long?"

"She's been in the hospital about two months," Megan said. "Actually it's not exactly a hospital. It's more a sort of rest home."

"Then she's not physically ill?"

"Oh, no. I mean, she's thin and run-down and all, but she doesn't have a disease or anything. It's all emotional. My little brother was killed last July. You may have read about it and seen his picture in the paper. Daniel Gregg?"

"I think I did," Julie told her, feeling the old, familiar sickness rising in her throat.

"Well, Ma blamed herself for that. Danny was spending the night with a friend a couple of miles from here, and he and the other boy had a fight. Danny called Ma and said he wanted to come home, and she said no, she wouldn't go pick him up. She told him he'd just have to stay there and work things out with his friend. But he wouldn't. He got on his bike and started home by himself. It was late at night, and the bike wasn't fixed for night riding. Somebody came roaring around the bend and smacked right into him."

"And you don't know who it was?" Julie found that her hands were shaking. She gripped one of the clothespins hard and pulled it off the sheet.

"The police think it might have been teenagers coming down from the Silver Springs picnic ground. There were some kids up there partying that night; one of the rangers saw them. He said there were four of them, two boys and two girls, but he didn't see them up close enough to begin to describe them. The emergency operator said the voice that called her sounded like a teenage boy, but she couldn't be certain either."

"And your mother?" Julie asked, taking her two corners of the sheet.

"She just sort of fell apart. It wasn't so bad at first. I guess we were all in shock. Danny was the littlest one, you see, the only child of Ma's second marriage and we all doted on him and kind of spoiled him. That's why Ma wouldn't pick him up that night. She and Pa had agreed they'd better stop giving in to him on everything he wanted. Then when he came on by himself and got killed, you can imagine how she felt. She blamed herself."

"But she couldn't have known what would happen!" Julie exclaimed.

"No, of course, she couldn't. We kept telling her that. But she dwelled on it, and pretty soon she had herself convinced that she'd all but killed Danny herself by not going to get him when he wanted her to. Then, a couple of months ago, she snapped. I mean, a morning came, and she couldn't get out of bed. She just lay there and she wouldn't talk to Pa or me. We called a doctor and, well…I won't go on with details. She's away now where she can get help."

"It's awful," Julie said. "Just awful." Her voice trembled slightly. She glanced toward the house. Where was Ray? Why was he taking so long?

Come on, please, she begged him silently. *Please come and get me out of this. I don't want to listen anymore.*

"Danny was a sweet kid," Megan was saying as she folded a shirt and laid it neatly in the basket on top of the sheet. "Stubborn, sure, but nice. He'd do anything for you if you asked him. He called me 'Sissy.' He started that back when he couldn't say 'sister.' I think about him a lot."

She glanced at Julie and stopped suddenly at the sight of her face. "I'm upsetting you, aren't I? Forgive me. Here you are, a perfect stranger, and I'm rattling on about all the family problems as though you were part of them."

"I'm just so terribly sorry for you. For all of you." Julie could hardly get the words out.

"It's more than that." Megan reached over and touched her hand. "I bet you've lost someone too, haven't you? I can tell. A brother or sister?"

"I'm an only child," Julie said. "But I did lose my father. It's been many years now."

"It does get easier, doesn't it? It must."

"It fades," Julie told her. "You stop thinking about it all the time, but you never ever really forget. I was just a little girl when Daddy died, but even now, when it's six o'clock and other fathers are coming home from work, I'll find myself glancing at the front door. One evening Bud—this guy I date—stopped by around that time, and I was sitting in the living room and heard his footsteps coming up the walk. He has a walk like Daddy's used to be, a kind of double-time stride—" She broke off as Ray appeared in the kitchen doorway. "Here! We're out here."

"I had to try calling a couple of places," Ray said. Julie could see by his eyes that the lie did not come easily. "I finally got somebody. He's on his way."

"There's a glass of iced tea for you over there on the table," Megan said.

"Thanks a lot, but I think we'd better get back to the car." He turned to Julie. "Are you ready?"

"Yes." *Oh, yes,* she added silently, *yes, yes, yes.* "Megan, thank you."

"Why, you're welcome. Selfishly, I'm glad you did have car trouble. I've been dying for somebody to talk to."

"I hope your mother gets better soon," Julie said, thinking how inadequate the words were.

"I believe she will. She has good doctors. And, of course, she has Pa there with her." The girl smiled warmly. "Come to the Bon Marche someday and let me do your hair for you. It's such a pretty color, it would be fun to work with."

"Thank you. Maybe I will." She felt Ray's hand on her arm. "Goodbye."

"Goodbye. I hope there's nothing too serious wrong with your car!" Megan called after them as they started toward the road.

They did not speak until they were in the car. Ray turned the key in the ignition and started the engine.

"The two of you sure got friendly fast," he said in a low voice. "What's the bit about her mother?"

"Megan's the Greggs' daughter," Julie told him, keeping her voice low so that it could not possibly carry back to the girl in the yard behind them. "Mrs. Gregg holds herself responsible for Daniel's accident. She's had a breakdown and is in a hospital south of here."

"Oh, god," Ray said painfully. "It never ends, does it?"

"Mr. Gregg's down there with her," Julie continued. "And Megan's here alone. Ray—" She fought to keep back the tears that were just beneath the surface. "We didn't just kill a little boy. We wrecked a whole family!"

"Every life is entwined with other people's," Ray muttered. "Like Barry's is with his parents' and Helen's, and even with ours. Are you sorry we came here?"

"Yes," Julie said. "I wish I didn't know. Before, these people were just names in a newspaper article. Now they're real. I'll never get Megan out of my mind, standing there, taking down laundry, talking about her little brother and how he used to call her 'Sissy.'" She raised her hand and wiped the back of it across her eyes. "There's one thing, though. We can be sure now that the Greggs didn't have anything to do with what happened to Barry."

"How do you get that?" Ray asked.

"Well, Megan couldn't have, not the way she acted with us. And her parents aren't here. They've been down in Las Lunas for months now."

"She told you that?"

"Yes. That's why she acted so lonesome. She's living here all by herself."

"That's funny," Ray said. "That house trim has been painted all the way up to the peak of the roof. She's such a short little thing, I don't see how she could reach that far."

"Perhaps a neighbor's helping her," Julie suggested. She was surprised at his observation. "What difference does it make?"

"None, I guess," Ray said. "But there's something else that bothers me. If she's living there alone, why were a man's shirts hanging on the line?"

"Maybe she wears them herself. A lot of girls wear their father's shirts to mess around in. I don't, of course, because I don't have a father, but a lot of my friends do."

"Okay," Ray said. "Okay, you've made your point." Julie could see that her nervous chatter was beginning to irritate him.

"I liked Megan," she said in a small voice. "I really did, Ray, and I think that Megan liked me."

"That doesn't mean that her father isn't capable of picking up a gun and shooting somebody. You've told me that Daniel was Mr. Gregg's only natural child. Megan and any other kids in the family are children from Mrs. Gregg's previous marriage. A man in that position would have a damned good reason for going off his rocker."

"But, her father's not there! He hasn't been there for months! Don't you believe that?"

"I don't know," Ray said wearily. "I honestly don't know what I believe anymore."

CHAPTER 11

They were on North Madison now, and with a practiced hand Ray spun the wheel to turn the car into the parking lot of the Four Seasons Apartments.

It was the first occasion he had had to call on anyone who lived in this apartment complex. He had to admit to himself that he was impressed as he followed Julie around the pool and up the steps to the level of second-floor apartments.

"Helen really seems to have hit the big time," he murmured as Julie pressed the buzzer beside the door of number 215.

She nodded. "Wait until you see the inside!"

The interior of the apartment was done in blues and greens and several shades of lavender. The cool colors were a perfect backdrop for Helen herself, who, unlike Julie, seemed to have changed little during the past year except, perhaps, to have grown even prettier.

She was glad to see them, almost too glad, grasping their hands in greeting and giving Ray a quick, welcoming kiss on the cheek.

"How great to see you! You look fantastic, Ray, all tanned and shaggy. I love men with beards."

She led the way through the foyer into the living room where a pale, heavy-set girl was seated on the sofa.

"Elsa," Helen said, "this is Ray Bronson, a friend from high school. I think you already know Julie James. Ray, my sister, Elsa."

"Glad to meet you, Elsa," Ray said politely, privately deciding just the opposite. He had seldom been introduced to anyone whose appearance made her less pleasing to meet. It seemed incredible on looking at her that this dumpy, sullen-faced girl could be closely related to someone as attractive as Helen.

"Hi," Elsa said. "Hello, Julie. Have you been sick or something? You sure don't look like you used to."

"I've lost a little weight, I guess," Julie said.

"Sit down," said Helen. "Let me get you a beer or a Coke or something."

"Thanks, but we didn't plan to stay very long." Julie made no move to take a seat. "We just thought we'd stop by to see what you'd heard about Barry. We didn't know you'd have company."

"Oh, don't worry about me," Elsa said. "I was just getting ready to leave anyway." She spread her legs apart, shifted her weight forward, and got heavily to her feet. "I came by for the same reason. When I read that article in the morning paper, I couldn't believe it. I said to Mom, 'That's Barry Cox who got shot! That's Helen's boyfriend!' I said, 'I'd better stop over after work and see how Helen's taking it.' I thought she'd be a wreck."

"I was one last night," Helen said, "when Collie drove me down to the hospital."

"Collie?" Elsa's sharp little eyes brightened with interest. "Who's that?"

"A nice guy who lives down the hall. He heard the report on TV and knew how I'd take it, so he came down to the studio to get me. The Coxes were there at the hospital, and Barry was in surgery, and they didn't know if he was going to live or not. It was awful. But today things are better."

"I called the hospital this morning," Ray said. "They wouldn't tell me much, but they did say he was out of recovery."

"I called too, and then again this afternoon."

"I'm surprised that you're not down there with him now," Elsa commented. "After all, to hear you talk, you're practically engaged to the guy."

"Barry needs his rest. I'll be going down to see him later." There was a note of strain in Helen's voice. "Thanks for coming by, Elsa. It was nice of you."

"Well, of course I came! My sister's boyfriend, shot in the

stomach! It's like something out of a movie. You think of things like this happening in New York City and Chicago and places like that, not in peaceful towns with normal people." Reluctantly, Elsa began to move in the direction of the door.

Helen stepped ahead of her to open it.

"Oh, by the way," Elsa paused again, "Mom says to ask you if you want to come home for a couple of days. You know, move back into the old homestead where she can feed you and give you hot tea and stuff. She's afraid you won't eat over here by yourself."

"No. Tell her thank you, but I'm doing fine." Helen held the door open wider. "Goodbye. Give my love to the rest of the family, and thanks again for coming over."

"That's okay. Like I said, it's just terrible. Mom will be calling you tonight, I guess, since you don't want to come home. She's worried about how you're taking this. Goodbye, Julie, you take care of yourself. It's nice to have met you, Ray."

The words kept coming as Elsa moved through the door and out onto the terraced hallway and only ended when Helen pushed the door closed behind her and leaned against it with an expression of exaggerated exhaustion.

"Thank god!" she said with a sigh of relief. "I was never so glad to see anybody in my life as I was when you two walked in. I was afraid I'd be stuck with her here all night."

"She sure doesn't bear much resemblance to you," Ray commented. "Are you sure you're really from the same family?"

"Too sure. Why do you think I was in such a hurry to move

into my own place? It wasn't to get away from my parents. I grew up sharing a room with Elsa." Helen left the door and came back into the living room to collapse onto the sofa that her sister had just vacated. "She was waiting here for me when I came back from the studio, and she's been here ever since, going over and over every grim detail and asking the most awful questions. I actually think she's enjoying the situation. She's never liked Barry anyway, and now she gets to brag to everybody in the store where she works that her almost-brother-in-law was shot down in cold blood."

"Are you really going down to the hospital tonight?" Ray asked her. "Are they allowing visitors?"

"Only family, and I don't qualify. At least, I didn't when I asked about it this morning." Helen made a gesture of frustration. "I just told that to Elsa to get her off my back. I ought to be able to see him."

"You certainly should," agreed Julie. "Can't the Coxes take you in with them when they go?"

"Are you kidding?" Helen said ruefully. "That's the last way I'll ever get in. You can't believe the things Mrs. Cox said to me last night while Barry was in surgery. She practically ordered me out of the waiting room. She even accused me of making the phone call that brought him out onto the athletic field."

"Then you didn't make it?" Ray asked her. "When the paper said that he got a call from somebody—"

"I know. I read that too. But it wasn't me."

"Then I guess you don't know any more than we do," Ray said. "We were hoping you could clear up a lot of things for us."

"I can't. The only thing—" Her voice fell off.

"What?"

"Well, there's that magazine picture that was on my door and the note that somebody sent Julie."

"And the clipping that was sent to me," said Ray.

"A clipping?" Helen's eyes widened.

"The newspaper account of the accident. I got it in the mail on Saturday. Somebody went to all the trouble of cutting it out and saving it and sending it to me."

"And you think there's a connection between that and what happened to Barry?" Helen asked him. "Oh, there couldn't be! I don't want to believe that."

"Neither does Julie," said Ray. "She's doing everything she can to convince herself that there isn't."

"No," Julie said in a low voice. "No, I'm finally convinced, now that we know it wasn't Helen who made that call. Somebody had to have made it. But I don't believe it was one of the Greggs."

"Then who was it?" Ray demanded. "Can you come up with somebody else?"

"Not right off, but that doesn't mean there isn't somebody who hated Barry for some other reason entirely."

"That's impossible," Helen said. "Nobody could hate Barry."

"How do you know?" Julie asked her.

111

"I know Barry better than anybody. After all, I've been going out with him for two full years. He doesn't have an enemy in the world."

Julie opened her mouth as though to respond to the statement, thought better of it, and closed it again. She turned to Ray.

"What do you think we ought to do?"

"I vote we go to the police," Ray said, "and tell them the whole story. It's what we should have done in the beginning."

"The police!" Helen exclaimed. "We can't do that, and you know it. We made a pact."

"Well, we can dissolve the pact," Ray said, "if the three of us agree to."

"I won't agree," Helen said. "Not ever. I think it's a shitty thing for you to suggest. Just because Barry's flat on his back in the hospital where he can't stand up for himself, you want to throw him to the wolves."

"That's not it at all!" Ray was beginning to get angry. "When we made the pact we never guessed that anything like this was going to happen. If the person who shot Barry did it for revenge, why should he stop with shooting one of the four of us? Next time it will be you or Julie or me."

"And if Barry wasn't shot for that reason, if it was just a crazy accident because some college freak was high and walking around waving a pistol, then you'd be reporting him for nothing. Barry would get out of the hospital and find himself facing a prison sentence. Hasn't he suffered enough without that?"

112

"Couldn't we talk to him?" Julie said. "He's bound to know what happened."

"How do you propose to get into the hospital to do that?" Helen asked bitterly. "If I can't see him, how can you?"

"Could we talk to him by phone?" Ray suggested.

"There's no phone in his room. I already asked."

"What about his parents?" asked Julie. "They get in to see him. Surely he must have told them who it was who called him right before he went out."

"They think it was me," Helen said.

"They may have thought that last night, but at that time they hadn't had a chance to talk with Barry. By now they may have learned the truth."

"I'll call and ask them," Ray volunteered.

"You?"

"Why not me? Barry and I have been friends for a long time. I tried to call his folks last night when I first heard about what happened, but they weren't there."

"Go ahead and try," Helen said. "There's nothing to lose. At least you may be able to find out more details about how he is."

"Fair enough." Ray got up and went over to the telephone. "Do you know the number?"

"It's on the front cover of the phone directory, written in red. The other number, the blue one, is the frat house."

Ray took the receiver off the hook and dialed. The phone was answered immediately by a low, male voice.

"Hello, Mr. Cox?" Ray said. "This is Raymond Bronson."

"Ray?" The man's voice sounded older than he remembered it. "Oh, yes, of course, Barry's friend. I didn't know you were still in town."

"I haven't been," Ray said. "I just got back from California a few days ago. I hadn't even had a chance to see Barry to say hi before I heard about the shooting. A bunch of his friends are real shaken up about it. I said I'd be the one to call you and see how things are going."

"He's going to pull through," Mr. Cox said. "There doesn't seem to be any doubt about that now. His mother and I were at the hospital this afternoon, and he seemed to have a good deal more strength than he had this morning."

"That's great," Ray said sincerely. "Do they think he'll be playing ball again next fall?"

"Well, that's something else again," Mr. Cox said slowly. "There's some question. You know the bullet lodged in his spine? Well, that's a tricky area. An injury there can cause paralysis."

"You mean, Barry might be paralyzed?!" Ray could not keep the horror from his voice.

"Not necessarily. We'll certainly pray not. At the moment that condition does seem to exist below the waist, but that could be only temporary. Of course, he hasn't been told anything about it. There's no sense in worrying him until he gets stronger, and by then there may be no need. He may be fine."

"I sure hope so," Ray said.

"We all do. You were kind to call, Ray. I'll tell Barry you're wishing him well."

"Please, do that. And, sir, I was wondering—do you suppose I might be able to see him?" In the light of what he had just been told, Ray asked it hesitantly. "It's been months since I saw him last, and I'd really like to talk with him."

"I'm afraid that's out of the question," Mr. Cox said firmly. "Barry's mother and I are the only visitors he's allowed to have. He's not up to socializing, as I'm sure you can understand. I'll pass along your good wishes."

"Mr. Cox?" Ray brought out the question quickly. "Have you had a chance, from anything he's said, to find out what actually happened? The phone call that the newspapers made such a big thing of, has he said who made that call to him? Is there any connection between that call and what happened after?"

"It seems very doubtful," Barry's father said. "According to Barry, that call was from Helen Rivers."

CHAPTER 12

"But Helen says it wasn't, and she should know if anybody does." Julie leaned her head against the back of the car seat with a sigh of such weariness that Ray turned to glance at her worriedly.

"You holding up okay there?"

"Oh, sure. I'm just fine. Just having a blast." She was frightened by the note of hysteria in her own voice. "Somebody's lying—Helen or Barry or Mr. Cox. Who is it, Ray? And why?"

They were driving back slowly through the gathering twilight. The mountains in the east were touched with pink from the last rays of the setting sun.

Somewhere up there, Julie thought, *is the Gregg's house, and Megan's there now, standing in the yellow kitchen, deciding whether it's worth it or not to fix a hot dinner for just one person. And a couple of miles north of that, the Silver Springs picnic area is growing cool and shadowy. Maybe later tonight there'll be a moon caught in that pine tree.*

"It's like a merry-go-round," she said wearily, "with everything going in circles and no answer to anything. Why would any one of the three of them lie?"

"Maybe they're all telling the truth."

"But how can they be, when the stories are different?"

"I don't mean telling the real truth," Ray said, "I mean the truth as they see it. Mr. Cox could be repeating exactly what Barry told him. Barry could have believed the person on the phone was Helen, even if it wasn't."

"You mean, somebody imitating Helen's voice?" Julie thought about that for a moment. "I suppose it's possible, though, he knows her so well...."

"He was expecting her to call him. She'd called earlier that day and left word for him to phone her and he hadn't. If the person on the phone was a girl or woman, somebody who knew Helen well and was able to copy her voice, and if Barry was expecting it to be Helen, he could have been fooled."

"But who would do such a thing?" Julie asked, and then suddenly a thought occurred to her. "Elsa!"

"Helen's sister?"

"Why not? She's a horrid person and obviously as jealous of Helen as she can possibly be. I remember the first day I met her—"

Her voice trailed off as her mind flew back to that bright

spring day just over a year ago, when she had walked home from school with Helen to see her prom dress.

It had seemed strange at the time to be going over to Helen's. Despite the fact that they dated boys who went around together, the girls themselves had little in common. Helen was not a girl for confidences and easy friendships and she took little interest in school activities. Julie, on the other hand, was almost *too* involved with clubs and committees and cheerleading practices to have time for a close, consuming relationship with any one particular person.

On this day, however, Helen had stopped her in the hall.

"I've got a dress for the prom," she had said excitedly. "Do you want to come over and see it?"

Her eyes had been shining, and her face had held the delighted look of a child who wants to share a marvelous treasure.

It had been impossible not to smile back at her.

"Sure," Julie had said, making a quick decision to skip the dance committee meeting, which was scheduled for after school. "I'd love to see it."

So they had met at the south door and had walked together through the soft, blue afternoon — an afternoon, Julie remembered now with a twinge of pain, so much like this one, except that there had been nothing to mar it. It had been a day filled with sunshine and plans for the coming dance and the wonder of being young and pretty and in love.

Helen's house had been small and shabby and overrun

with children. Two little boys had been fighting in the front yard, and a blaring TV set had dominated the living room where a solemn-faced girl of about twelve and a toddler in a wet diaper had sat mesmerized.

Helen's mother had been in her bedroom.

"She's not feeling too good," Helen had remarked matter-of-factly. "The noise and the yelling and everything gets to her when she's pregnant. Come on, my room's at the back of the house."

That was where she had met Elsa. A heavily built girl, apparently a couple of years older than Helen, she had been sprawled upon one of the twin beds, leafing through a magazine. She had glanced up at them as Julie and Helen had come in, and her eyes had narrowed a little behind her glasses.

"Don't tell me," she had said, "the Princess is actually bringing home a girlfriend!"

"This is my sister, Elsa," Helen had said. "This is Julie James."

"The cheerleader." Elsa's voice had been flat. "We hear about Julie James all the time around here, her and Barry Cox and the other high-class people Helen runs around with."

"Hello, Elsa," Julie had said as pleasantly as she could. Her eyes rested on the dress that was spread out across Helen's neatly made bed. "Oh, isn't it beautiful!"

It was, too. Simple and white with flowing Grecian lines and a thin gold thread running along the edge. As Helen had lifted the dress and held it up in front of her, Julie had caught her breath at the effect.

"It's gorgeous!" she had exclaimed. "Just elegant! Where in the world did you find it?"

There was a moment's silence, and then Elsa said, "Well, speak up, Helen. Aren't you going to tell her?" She turned to Julie. "She got it at the thrift shop. That's where she gets all her 'elegant' clothes. They're things other people don't want. That dress probably belonged to some society lady who got too fat to wear it."

"You didn't have to say that, Elsa." Helen's face turned bright red and she lowered the dress, holding it defensively in front of her as though to shield herself from the words. "It doesn't look like it's from a thrift shop."

"I think it's wonderful that you found it," Julie said quickly. "It doesn't matter where it came from. I'm sure it looks better on you than it ever could have looked on anybody else. If that's the sort of thing you can find at the thrift store, I'm going to start shopping there too."

"I don't always," Helen said. "Most of the time I go to regular stores. It's just that formals are so expensive."

"And our lovely Helen can't look like everybody else — she's got to be a princess." Elsa sat up on the bed. She spoke quietly, but there was a bitterness in her voice that made Julie wince.

"This is my day off, Monday. A great time for a day off, isn't it? What can you do on a Monday? The rest of the week I'm standing on my feet all day behind the lingerie counter at

Wards. For what? To bring home enough money so that Mom can turn right around and hand Helen enough to buy a prom dress that she'll wear one time and stick in the back of the closet."

"It didn't cost very much," Helen said.

"Then why didn't you earn the money for it? Why can't you get an after-school job and put some cash in instead of taking it out? That fast-food place on Carlisle is looking for kitchen help during the supper hour. All you'd have to do is apply."

"I don't want to cook hamburgers, thank you. I do enough of that here." Helen went over and hung the dress in the closet. "Come on," she said to Julie, "let's go get a soda or something."

"I can't," Julie had said, glancing self-consciously at her watch. "I've got to get home. Ray's coming over."

She had smiled at Elsa. It had not been easy.

"Goodbye," she had said. "It's been nice meeting you."

"Likewise," Elsa had answered.

Reaching back now in her mind, that was the picture that Julie had retained of Elsa: heavy-legged, square-faced, hair matted from the pillow, a slight double chin, and those sharp eyes, glaring through the glasses, and the bitterness, the terrible bitterness.

"She could have done it," she said now to Ray. "She could have called Barry and pretended to be Helen. She could even have shot him."

"You think so?" Ray sounded skeptical. "She's a mess, I'll

agree with that, but what's she got against Barry? You don't go out and shoot your sister's boyfriend for no reason."

"Jealousy," Julie said. "By hurting Barry, she'd be hurting Helen."

"I guess it's possible. And the cover-up with the notes and stuff to you and me. She could have learned about the accident. Helen said they used to share a bedroom. Maybe Helen talks in her sleep or something."

They had reached the James' house now. Ray pulled up in front, leaving the motor running.

"You want me to come over later? We could talk."

"I think we've talked enough," Julie said. "My head's churning now, and I don't see how hashing it over any further will help. The person we need to talk with is Barry."

"Well, maybe by tomorrow we can." Ray moved as though to touch her, then thought better of it and put his hand back on the wheel. "Take care."

It was not a casual goodbye. His eyes were worried.

"I mean it, Jules. Please, be careful."

"You mean, watch out?"

"Yes. And don't go rushing out to meet somebody who phones or, you know.... We can't be sure it was Elsa. We can't be sure of anything right now. So take care. Okay?"

"You too," Julie said. "You take care too."

She got out of the car. The dark was beginning to close in quickly. The sky had faded from pink to purple, and one lone star twinkled directly above her. The house lights were on, and when she reached the steps she looked back to see that Ray was still parked there, watching her. It wasn't until she was inside with the door closed behind her that she heard the engine rev and the car pull away.

Her mother was baking again. A bread smell filled the house.

"Julie?" she called from the kitchen. "Is that you, honey?"

"Sure. Who else?"

For a long moment she stood in the living room, bracing herself, trying to calm the beating of her heart. Emotional exhaustion from the afternoon's confrontations threatened to overwhelm her. The warm comfort of the house, her mother's welcoming voice, the safe, familiar odors and sounds and feel of home were suddenly more than she could bear.

"Julie? I'm in the kitchen."

"Be right there." Drawing a deep breath to stabilize herself, Julie went through the living room and out into the kitchen.

Her mother, who was removing bread from the loaf pan, glanced at her casually and then not so casually. Her eyes were questioning.

"What is it, dear? Is something wrong?"

"No. What could be wrong?" Julie motioned toward the bread. "What's all this baking bit lately? Are you trying to turn us both into elephants?"

"A few extra pounds wouldn't hurt you in the slightest." Her mother turned back to the job at hand. "Where in the world have you been? It's after six thirty."

"Ray picked me up after school. We rode around and talked."

"That's nice." Her mother smiled. "I'm glad Ray's back. I just wish he'd shave off that silly beard and look like himself again."

"I sort of like the beard," Julie said. "He seems older with it."

"I noticed that too, but it's more than the beard, I think. That year in California matured him a lot. I've always been fond of Ray, as you know, but when I was talking with him yesterday evening, before you got back from Helen's, it was like talking to another adult." Mrs. James laughed. "I don't suppose either of you would consider that much of a compliment."

"That's funny," Julie said. "You like it that Ray seems older, but with Bud, who really is a little bit older, you don't like it at all."

"Well, there's older, and then there's older. Bud acts like my grandfather. I'm willing to bet he proposes before he so much as kisses you good night."

"I'll let you know. He hasn't done either one yet."

Julie stood, leaning against the doorframe, watching her mother transfer the bread loaf onto a plate. The overhead light caught her hair in a glint of silver.

Wow, that's gray, Julie thought, startled. *She's turning gray.*

She stood frozen, staring at her mother's hair, always so thick and dark. "Like raven wings," her father had said once, reaching out a gentle hand to stroke the shining richness. When had it begun to change? Yesterday? Last week? Last year?

Wrapped up as she had been in her own concerns, she had not noticed.

The veins stood out like thin purple cords on the backs of her mother's hands as she lifted the cake lid to set it over the plate. They were no longer a young woman's hands.

"Mom." Julie spoke softly, swept by a wave of tenderness so great that it bordered on pain. "Mom, I love you so much."

"Why, honey!" Her mother turned to her in surprise. "I love you too. Julie, what is it, dear? Something is wrong."

For one crucial instant Julie wavered, torn by the temptation to step forward and throw herself into her mother's arms to weep out the whole dreadful story. What comfort there would be in letting it all out at last! To lean upon an adult shoulder, to cry, "I have done an awful thing! I have been part of an awful thing!" To plead, "Help me, Mom! Tell me what I should do!" seemed at that moment the closest thing to heaven.

But she did not do it, stopped as much by the vulnerability of her mother's face as by the memory of the pact. This was a woman who had borne enough burdens. The responsibility was Julie's, not her mother's, and pain shared in this case would not be pain lessened.

So she merely said, "I'm tired, I guess. Exams and everything, and the excitement about being accepted at Smith. Do you want me to start fixing dinner? Did you have something special planned?"

"I thought we'd just microwave something frozen,"

Mrs. James said. "With home-baked bread, what more do we need?"

The telephone rang.

Bud's voice said, "You must have been talking to somebody pretty fascinating. I've been getting a busy signal for over an hour."

"There must be something wrong with the line," Julie told him. "We have trouble like that sometimes. A couple of months ago our phone was out for three days and we didn't even know it."

"Well, I'm glad I finally got you," Bud said. "I thought you might want to go to a movie tomorrow night. You've been studying too hard. A little R and R might be good for you."

"Only if it's a comedy," Julie said. "Something heavy and dramatic would finish me off."

They talked for a few minutes, and Julie agreed to a date the following evening. By the time she came back to the kitchen, she had control of herself again.

Though her mother kept glancing at her worriedly during dinner, their conversation was normal, and that one instant in which the whole story had almost come rushing out was securely behind her.

CHAPTER 13

The woman in the crisp, white uniform set the vase of carnations on the window ledge and looked at the card.

"This one's from Crystal," she said. "She says, 'Get well fast, it doesn't seem the same without you.'" She glanced up and gestured to the other containers of flowers crowding the sill and the bedside table and lining the wall along the far side of the room.

"This place is like a hothouse. How many girlfriends do you have, anyway?"

"Enough," Barry said shortly.

This was his least favorite of the nurses. She was young, hardly older than he was, and pretty in a crisp, efficient way. She was the sort of girl he might have made a play for if he had met her somewhere else, coming on strong with the football hero routine and knocking her off her feet. The fact that she should have him here at her disposal, flat on his back, helpless, was infuriating.

He turned his head and shut his eyes, pretending that he was going to sleep, and after a moment he heard the swish of her skirts as she left the room.

It was Wednesday. They had told him that this morning. At first he had refused to believe it—what had happened to Tuesday? And then bits and pieces of Tuesday had begun to come back to him: the ride on a gurney down the long corridor, the transfer onto this bed, his father's lined face looking down at him. The latter part of Tuesday came into sharper focus. His mother weeping. A needle in his arm. A needle in his hip. The doctor with the white hair. The doctor with the black hair.

Surprisingly, he did not recall a great deal of pain.

"He's sedated," the doctor with the black hair had said when his father bent over him, trying to ask him questions, but he had not been so doped up that he had not known what the questions were.

"It was Helen," he had said, and his father had been satisfied.

"He says the call was from Helen," he had told someone behind him, and Barry had heard his mother's voice exclaiming, "It would have been, of course. I knew that girl was trouble the first time I saw her."

This morning his mind had been clearer, and he had been able to take things in: the pile of cards on the bedside table, the flowers on the sill, the identity of the nurses as they changed shifts. He was terribly weak; he discovered that when he reached out his hand for the Get Well card on the top of the pile and found that it was shaking so much that he could not open the envelope.

But the pain was less than he would have expected, considering a bullet had gone practically all the way through him.

"I can't feel my legs at all," he had said to the doctor, the white-haired one this time, who had come in to change the dressing.

"They're there," the doctor had told him crisply. "Two of them. Were you maybe looking for a third?"

The sweetheart roses were from Helen. "With all my love," the card said, and she had signed it, "Heller," his own private name for her. It was exactly the way she had signed her junior class picture, the photo that was lying back at the fraternity house facedown on top of his dresser.

He wished there were some way for Helen to know he turned over that picture. He wished she could know that he was through with her before this shooting ever took place. It was one thing to reach the decision that it was time to break up with a girl who was getting to be a drag. It was another thing entirely to find the decision made for you, to discover that the girl you had supposed to be honest, clinging and all-adoring had in reality been two-timing you.

"Helen has called to ask about you several times," his father had told him this morning.

"And she and a friend came down to the hospital Monday night," his mother had added. "I think that was in questionable taste. They got the news from a TV report."

"She came with a friend?" Barry had asked. "You mean with Julie?"

"No, with a boyfriend. Dark-haired. Not too tall. Collie Something-or-other she called him. They seemed to know each other very well."

His mother had reached over and taken his hand.

"I know this isn't the right time to tell you this, dear, but is there ever such a thing as a 'right time'? I just don't want you to lean emotionally on a relationship that apparently is unstable."

"There isn't any 'relationship,'" Barry had told her grimly. "Helen's free to date anybody she wants." But the revelation had knocked the breath out of him.

Of all the lousy tricks, he had raged silently. *Two whole years of the faithful, loving, I'm-yours-forever bit, and all the time she's had some other guy on the side. The lying bitch! And then she had the nerve to bring him to the hospital with her!*

If only he had gotten there first. He should have been the one to break things off, standing straight and firm on his own two feet with some other girl on his arm, while Helen cried and pleaded and begged for another chance. But, no, he had been

130

too worried about hurting her, and he had missed that opportunity. Now here he was, flat in bed, unable to take even a flimsy poke in return, while his mother brought him the news and enjoyed every minute of it.

"Take those roses and shove them," he had told the stout, red-faced nurse who had been on duty when the flowers arrived, but she had not done so. She had placed them instead behind some other vases, and he could see them now, peeking out in all their pink innocence, from the far side of a shaggy, green plant. If it had been possible for him to have gotten out of bed and crossed the room to reach them, he would have smashed them to a pulp.

But he could not even do that. He could only lie here and fume and hate everybody—Helen, the boyfriend, the doctors, and the whole damned world. Which included his mother. She had him down at last, and there was no way of getting away from her ministrations. It was not so bad when his father was here too, but this morning, after a brief look-in and a "How are you feeling today, son?" he had gone on to the office and left his wife behind. She had settled into the chair by Barry's bed with the satisfaction of a mother hen hopping into its nest, and after two full hours of her chatter he had been ready to shout for a shot, a pill, anything that would shut off the sound of her voice.

"We're getting your old room ready for you to come home to," she had told him. "I thought I'd have the walls painted a pale green. Don't you think that would be a nice, restful color? And we can put the portable TV in there, and your computer. Dad's going down to the University tomorrow to pick up your things. Your friend Lou is going to have them all packed for us, so they'll be waiting at home for you when you get there."

"You make it sound like I'm coming home forever." Barry had tried to conceal the panic that came with voicing the thought. "I'm not, you know. As soon as this hole in my stomach heals up and I can eat solid stuff again and get my strength back, I'll be up and out. I've still got Europe in mind for this summer, though I guess it will have to be the end of the summer now."

"I know, dear," his mother had said, and there had been a funny note in her voice. "Still, while you are at home with us, it will be nice to have a pleasant room to stay in, won't it?"

She did not argue about the proposed European trip, nor did she repeat her earlier suggestion about the family car trip to the East Coast. This omission in itself was disconcerting and, in a way, almost frightening.

Aside from his parents, Barry was being allowed no visitors, and that was how he wanted it. Having his mother constantly there was strain enough without adding a troop of frat brothers and a barrage of weeping females. As the irritating little nurse had commented, enough of them had sent flowers to open a flower shop. He could imagine the scene with all of them—Crystal and Madison and two-faced Helen and the rest—drifting in and out in a never-ending stream, wringing their hands and bringing him books to read and having to be introduced to each other as they met across his bed.

Even Julie had sent a plant with a note on it saying, "Get well fast. We're thinking about you." Who "we" was he wasn't sure—herself and Helen, perhaps, or Ray or somebody else. He couldn't care less.

"Hey, Barry?" The voice was an echo of his last thought, a familiar voice but one that he had not heard in a long time. "Are you asleep?"

Barry jerked open his eyes.

"What are you doing here?"

"I came up the back stairs," Ray said, "and just walked down the hall and in the door. I passed some nurses but nobody stopped me."

"They should have. Don't you know I'm not supposed to have visitors?"

"Yeah, I know, and I'll probably get thrown out in a couple of minutes. How's it going?" Curious despite himself, Barry studied the face of the boy who stood at the end of his bed. In the months since he had last seen him, Ray had changed tremendously. He looked broader through the shoulders and chest and, somehow, older. He was very tan, and the beard gave character to a face that always before had held a not-quite-finished look, like a portrait by an artist who had not been able to decide what to do with the mouth and chin. Now the face was done and, young as it was, it was a man's face.

133

The eyes were steady and direct and they softened with sympathy.

"It's going great," Barry said sarcastically. "I was needing a nice vacation. How are things with you?"

Ray came around and stood by the side of the bed, looking down at him. *Crazy,* Barry thought. He'd never had Ray look down at him before. He had always been the one to look down. He knew the top of Ray's head by heart.

"God, Barry, I'm sorry," Ray was saying. "I'm sorry as hell. This is a shitty thing to have happen. Are you in a lot of pain?"

"It isn't exactly a picnic," Barry said. "What did you come here for?"

"Well, to see how you were, for one thing. All your friends have been calling the hospital, but they don't tell us much. I talked to your dad yesterday, and I hated to keep bugging him."

"What did he say?" Barry asked.

"That you were over the hump. Getting better. Able to see the family. Stuff like that."

"Did he say anything about my legs?" Barry saw a shadow flicker across the green eyes. There was a slight hesitation before Ray answered.

"No."

"You're lying," Barry said flatly.

"I'm not. I didn't talk with him very long. He said you were going to be okay."

134

"I'll just bet he did." *I hate him,* Barry thought. *I hate him lying to me, patronizing me, standing here on his two good legs, able to turn around and walk out of here whenever he wants to. I wish somebody would shoot a bullet into his guts so he'd know what it was like to lie on the ground in the dark and yell and not have anybody hear you.*

Aloud he said, "How was it in California?"

"Good in some ways, not so good in others." Ray sounded relieved at the change in topic. "I did a lot of thinking while I was out there. There's something about being alone with no one to fall back on. You start learning how to fall back on yourself. You settle down in your mind and get your thinking into balance. You know what I mean?"

"What sort of thinking?" Barry asked him warily.

"Oh, about right and wrong and responsibility and what's important. Stuff like that. Look, what I'm getting at—"

"I know what you're getting at," Barry interrupted. "You want to blow the whistle on me about that accident. Right?"

"I don't want to blow any whistle," Ray said. "I just think we went off the deep end too fast. We were all shaken up that night, and we made a decision we shouldn't have made, and now I think we ought to consider it again."

"Go ahead and consider it," Barry told him. "Consider it all you want to. You can't break the pact."

"We could dissolve the pact."

"Only if we all agree, and I don't."

"Barry, look." Ray drew closer to the bed and lowered his voice. "It's more than just a moral thing; it's for our own safety.

135

Somebody's got our number—how, we don't know—but somebody does, and whoever it is put a bullet through you the other night. You were lucky. You lived through it. But who's to say he's not going to try it again when you get out of here?"

"When I get out of here," Barry said, "I'm not going to be within range of any hothead with a gun. I'm going to be flat on my back at home in a 'nice, restful' newly painted green bedroom with my mom standing guard at the door."

"Then think about the rest of us. Think about Helen."

"You think about Helen if you want to; I'd rather not. And if you see her you can tell her to stop bothering my folks with phone messages. Girls like her are a dime a dozen, and I happen to have a pocket full of dimes."

"Barry, listen—"

"No, you listen," Barry said savagely. "Somebody shot me, yes, but that doesn't mean it had anything to do with that car accident. That's old stuff. It's over. This was something entirely different."

"How do you know?" Ray asked. "Did you see who did it?"

"No, but I know why he did it. I had fifty bucks in my wallet when I left the house that night. When they brought me in here, I didn't have any cash left."

"You mean it was robbery?" Ray exclaimed doubtfully.

"Yes, it was robbery. What else?"

"But what about the phone call? The papers said you got a call right before you went out. A couple of the guys at the

136

frat house heard you talking to somebody, promising to meet her. Your dad says it was Helen. Helen says it wasn't."

"It wasn't," Barry said. "I told that to Dad because it was the easiest thing to say. I didn't want to mess things up any more than they already were. This girl I was talking to is a real hot little number. I've been seeing her for a long time now, but I didn't want to hurt Helen by having her find out about it."

"This girl called and wanted you to meet her on the athletic field? Why?"

"I wasn't meeting her there," Barry told him. "I was just crossing the field because it was the shortest way to reach the stadium. I was going to meet her there. We were going to watch the fireworks and then go back to her place. So, I never got there. Tough luck for me."

"You swear that?" Ray said. "You swear it was another girl you were dating?"

"Sure, I swear it, and you can tell Helen if you want to. Let her face reality for a change. I've got plenty of girls on the hook. Helen's just one of them."

"Then this had nothing to do with the Gregg kid?"

"That's what I'm telling you. They're two different things. You turn me in for the Gregg kid, and all you're doing is kicking me when I'm down. I swear, Ray, if you do that to me I'll never forgive you. We made a pact."

"Okay," Ray said softly. "Okay. Simmer down. I didn't mean to get you so riled up."

137

"What do you expect, throwing something like that at me?" Barry was riled up. His head was throbbing and the whole room was beginning to move out of focus. "Look, how about getting out of here? I'm not supposed to see people and I don't feel so great."

"Sure. I'm sorry." Ray touched his shoulder. "I really am sorry. Get better, okay?"

"Yeah. Sure."

Barry closed his eyes, and the room went swinging around beyond the darkness of his eyelids.

Get out of here, he shouted silently. *Get out, get out, get out! Walk out of here on your good legs and go run around the block or something, you Brutus, you Judas, you faithful, loyal best friend of mine with your new "balanced" thinking and your "let's dissolve the pact." Get out and leave me alone!*

He wished he could be there to see Helen's face when Ray told her the story about the phone call. "It was a girl," he would say. "Somebody he's been seeing for a while now." That would show her. She might as well know that she hadn't quite made a fool of him. Maybe she was playing around on the side, but so was he, and a whole lot heavier than she was.

It could have been true. It could have been another girl-friend on the telephone. Crystal did sometimes call him, and so did some of the others. It could as easily have been one of them that night calling to ask him to meet her at the stadium.

Or it could have been Helen. That was whom he had

expected. That was why the strange voice had disconcerted him so completely.

"Cox here," he had said, and the voice, low-pitched and muffled, as though the speaker was talking through some cloth, had said, "Barry?"

"Hello? Who's this?"

"A friend," the voice had said. "A friend who knows about something and needs to talk to you about it."

"About what?" Barry had known that he was reacting stupidly, but he could think of nothing else to say. "What are you talking about?"

"I think you know. Something that happened last summer." There had been a pause. "What would you say if I told you I had a picture?"

"A picture of what?" Barry had asked, his stomach knotting.

"An action picture with a car in it. And a bicycle. Just part of the bicycle. Would you be interested in seeing it?"

"No," Barry had said. "I wouldn't."

"Perhaps there might be other people I could show it to." The voice had been calm and thoughtful. "Like, for instance, the boy's parents. I think they might be interested."

"You can't take good pictures at night." Barry had bitten before he could stop himself. Immediately, on realizing what he had done, he had been filled with fury at his own stupidity. "Who the hell are you, anyway?"

"Somebody who uses special film," the voice had told him. "A fast film that takes great shots in dim light, even less light than you get from headlights. I'm willing to make a deal with you. I'd like to sell this picture plus the negative. It wasn't taken digitally, and I haven't scanned it, so that will be the end of it. I'm not asking you to buy it sight unseen. I'm calling from here on campus. I can show you the picture."

"I'll just bet you can. There isn't any film like that." He had not been sure of his ground. He had never been interested in photography and knew little about it. "I'll believe it when I see it."

"Then I'll meet you over at the athletic field in about five minutes. Under the stands."

"That's fine with me," Barry had said. "You'd better be there." He had placed the receiver back on the hook and turned to the boys behind him. "It's all yours."

"Man," one of them had said, "if I talked to my girl like that, she'd shoot me!"

Funny, Barry thought now, *that he should have put it that way, like a premonition.* Keeping his eyes tightly closed, he thought about the place in the bed where his feet were lying. "They're there," the doctor had said, and they were, for he had seen the shape of them under the sheet, sticking up like blocks of wood.

So much for you, Ray Bronson, he felt like shouting. *Crashing in here, trying to pump me, making threats! So you came here to see how I was, did you? Like hell, you did! You came to get information to cover your ass. So you got it, but it wasn't what you expected, was it? Well, suppose you figure things out for yourself with all that good thinking you taught yourself to do while you were in California. Don't think I'm going to help you. I don't owe you anything.*

You figure things out for yourselves — you and Julie and Helen. It'll give you something to keep you busy in the evenings. As for myself, I've got plenty to do with chatting up pretty nurses and being put on and off bedpans and visiting with my mother. It's enough to keep me busy the rest of my life!

The words blurred in his head into one massive shout, and the hot tears finally came.

CHAPTER 14

Ray drew a long breath of relief as he passed through the swinging glass doors of the hospital lobby and stepped out into the warm flood of afternoon sunshine.

Well, that's that, he told himself. *Here I had myself all worked up, and there wasn't anything to be worried about. The attack on Barry was robbery, just robbery. Nothing to do with me or with Julie or even with Helen. Nobody's out to get any of us, at least not physically.*

The relief was so great that he felt light-headed with the intensity of it. As he walked down the sidewalk he had a crazy desire to turn to everyone he passed and shout out, "Hello there! We're okay! Everything's okay!"

Though, of course, it wasn't really. One terror out of the way did not mean that there were not things to be concerned about. A person existed who knew—or thought they knew—about last summer's accident. Though Barry had now erased for them the fear that this person was out for physical revenge, there still must be some plan behind the malicious notes and clippings. No actual threat had yet been made, but soon there would have to be something. Perhaps it would be blackmail, like "Pay me this much money, or I'll go to the police with my information."

If that happens, Ray thought, *I can go to the cops. That would be fine with me. I'm not going to hand over one dollar to get further into this mess than I am right now. If I had my way, I'd be headed straight for the police myself. If only I hadn't let myself be talked into that damned pact, if I'd listened to Julie that night instead of to Barry—*

But what was done was done. That night could not be re-lived by any of them. Neither could any of them dictate what was to take place from now on. Elsa—if, as Julie suspected, it was Elsa—would do that. The more he thought about it though, the harder it was for Ray to imagine Elsa in the role of blackmailer. There was nothing subtle about Elsa. If she had something to use against Helen, she would use it with full venom, he was certain, but the brains and patience necessary for this sort of cat-and-mouse play would be surprisingly out of character.

"Ray? Hey, you're Ray Bronson, aren't you?"

Ray was startled from his thoughts by a voice from behind him. He turned and for a moment stared without recognition at the dark-haired, square-built young man who had called out his name.

Then the realization struck him.

"Oh, hi," he said. "Bud, isn't it?"

"Right. I thought that was you, but I wasn't sure. I saw you come out of the hospital. You have somebody in there?"

"A friend," Ray said. "Barry Cox. Julie may have mentioned him to you."

"The guy who was shot over at the college?" The older boy nodded. "That was a tough break. How is he doing? Are they allowing him to have visitors?"

"No," Ray said. "I sort of crashed through the gates. He's doing okay, I guess, as okay as possible under the circumstances."

He made the statement with effort. The sight of Barry's long, strong body laid out flat and helpless in the hospital bed had shaken him severely. Ray had little experience with hospitals. He had never even been inside one except one time to see his mother when she was hospitalized after an appendectomy. That had been different. The operation had been successfully completed, his mother had been smiling, and they all had known that she would be home within a couple of days, strong and well and ready to throw herself back into the full joy of living.

With Barry, no such guarantee existed.

"Paralysis," Mr. Cox had said yesterday on the phone. "At the moment that condition does seem to exist, but it may only be temporary. Of course, he hasn't been told anything about it."

But he knows, Ray thought now. *Maybe they haven't told him, but he knows.* The knowledge had been there in Barry's eyes, and the bitterness in his voice had been only a thin mask over the sound of fear.

As though reading his mind, Bud said, "I hate hospitals." He had moved up to fall into step beside Ray. "I'm heading down to that Starbucks on the corner to pick up some coffee cake or something. Want to join me?"

"Well—" Ray hesitated. He had had lunch and was not particularly hungry. At the same time, he had to admit to himself a painful curiosity about the guy who appeared to have taken his place in Julie's life. She had said that she was not in love, but there had to be something in the relationship for her to continue to see him so regularly.

"Sure," he said. "I could use a cup of coffee."

When they entered the coffee shop, they found that it was almost deserted. Ray ordered a latte while Bud bought a croissant, then they selected a table. As they waited for the latte, Ray devoted himself to studying the face of the young man across from him. *What,* he wondered, *did Julie see in it? Was it a face that flashed into her mind as soon as she woke up in the morning? Did it have a place in her dreams at night?*

Bud was not exactly handsome, but he had an air of quiet self-confidence that a girl like Julie might find attractive. The cut of his hair and the fact that his face was closely shaven accentuated the several years between their ages. He had the strong jaw and direct, determined gaze of a young man who was used to setting a course and sticking to it.

145

If he decided he wanted a girl, Ray thought, *he wouldn't call it quits until he got her.* The observation was more than a little disturbing.

"Are you sure you don't want something besides coffee?" Bud asked.

"I'm sure," Ray said. "That hospital visit got to me. Barry was my best friend in high school. We're not so close now, but still...seeing him down flat like that—"

"I can imagine," Bud said. "Like I told you, I hate hospitals. Just the smell of one is enough to give me nightmares."

"Have you ever been in one?" Ray asked him.

"Yep. After Iraq." Bud didn't elaborate. "Say, what's Julie's connection with your friend? She told me she sent a plant over to the hospital. She doesn't date him, does she?"

"God, no," Ray told him. "She doesn't even like him much. We all used to hang out together—Julie and me and Barry and a girl named Helen Rivers. Then something happened and...well, we don't anymore."

"Helen Rivers." Bud repeated the name slowly. "That sounds familiar. Maybe Julie's mentioned her."

"You could have seen her on TV. She works for one of the local stations." Ray decided to ask the question that was uppermost in his mind. "Are you seeing a lot of Julie?"

"Quite a bit," Bud said. "Does that bother you?"

"Sure," Ray said wryly, "but there doesn't seem to be much I can do about it. She used to be my girlfriend, and I'd better warn you, I'm going to do everything I can to get her back."

"Are you now?" There was a hint of amusement in Bud's voice. "Well, you can try, but it's not that easy to go back and pick up a relationship once you've let it go down the drain. If Julie still means that much to you, why did you take off on her?"

"I didn't take off on her," Ray said. "I felt like I had to get away for awhile and do some thinking and kind of sort out the way I felt about things."

"Sounds like escapism to me," Bud said shortly. "Plain running away."

"It was," Ray admitted. "I know that now. That's why I came back."

"Expecting to find everything blown over and back to normal?"

"No. I didn't expect that." The subject was getting out of hand. Ray shifted uncomfortably. The last person in the world he had intended to spill his guts to was the guy who represented his competition for Julie.

"We had something pretty great going once," he said. "Julie and I. Maybe I can get her to give it another shot. Maybe I can't. It'll be up to her. I guess she told you, she's going east to college in a couple of months."

"And you're planning to follow her?"

"I wish I could, but I didn't apply to any of the Ivy League schools. Probably couldn't have gotten in if I had. I'll be staying here. I'm going to register at the University."

"You know what you're going to take?"

"I think so," Ray said. "I've got an idea anyway. I think I might go into education. I've always been pretty good at getting ideas across to people. Back in high school I tutored the whole damned football team to keep their grades high enough so they could play. I'm sure this won't go over well with my dad, but by now he's faced up to the fact that his son is not going to be a professional athlete. I'm sure he'd rather see me a teacher than a gas station attendant."

"I never would have thought of you as a kid-lover. Teaching is—" Bud interrupted himself. "There's your coffee."

There was a break in the conversation while Ray went to the counter to get his drink. Ray dumped sugar into his coffee and stirred it. He had the uncomfortable feeling that he had been talking too much to someone who, while not an enemy, was certainly not a friend. His whole purpose in having coffee with Bud Wilson was to find out more about the guy. So far he had done nothing except offer information about himself.

Returning to the table, he tried to turn the conversation in another direction. "You said you were in the hospital," he began. "Was that for a war injury?"

"I'd rather not talk about it." Bud closed that subject as quickly as it had been opened.

"I'm sorry," Ray said awkwardly.

"That's okay. It's just not something I like to talk about. War is hell, Bronson." Bud picked up his croissant and took a bite out of it. "Don't remember who said that. Somebody famous. Somebody who'd been through it. He laid it out pretty clearly with that short statement. It's bad enough shooting people and being shot at, but that's the military—you tell yourself you're there for that purpose, to kill people who are there to kill you—the army's arranged it for you, and the good old USA is behind it, so the whole thing's got the Good Housekeeping Seal of Approval....

"What gets to you is the kids. They don't even know what the fighting's about; they're just mixed up in it because it's happening where they live."

"Tough," said Ray, inadequately. There was a moment of silence. He took a swallow of coffee and wondered why he had ordered it; the thought of consuming a whole cup of the hot liquid was more than he could handle.

"Look," he said, "I've got to be going."

Bud seemed surprised. "But we just sat down."

"I know," Ray said. "I've got to make a phone call. It's something I should have done earlier. It just slipped my mind."

"If it's to Julie," Bud said, "don't bother. I'm taking her out tonight myself." He smiled. It was the first time he had smiled since they had sat down together. "I'll make you a bet about something, Bronson."

"What?" Ray asked.

"I'll bet you that Julie doesn't go to Smith in September."

"You're crazy," Ray told him. "Of course she's going. She's excited about it. What do you think will hold her back?"

"I will." Bud made the statement with simple assurance.

"She doesn't know it yet. It's a long three months between now and September."

"You're crazy," Ray said again as he got to his feet. "Julie isn't ready to settle down with anybody. She's not even eighteen yet. She's not going to stay in this town for you or for me or for anyone else."

"We'll see about that." Bud raised his hand in a friendly gesture of farewell. "It was good talking with you, Bronson. I'll be seeing you around."

"Sure," Ray said. "Be seeing you."

He stopped to leave a tip at the counter and then stepped out onto the sidewalk. He took out his cell, and punched in Julie's number. His call rang and rang, then went into voice-mail. "It's me," he said and clicked the "off" button, feeling unreasonably angry. Who could Julie be talking to this early in the afternoon? She had just left her school friends; there was nothing she would need to call them about. Or was the phone just turned off? If so, why? He assumed that she would have been eagerly waiting for him to call with the results of his talk with Barry.

His reaction was unreasonable, and he knew it. Julie had no idea that he was going to try to see Barry today or that he would be trying to call her. Whom she talked to after school was her own business, just as it was her own business with whom she went out in the evenings.

Except for this guy, Ray told himself helplessly. *I don't want her going out with him.* The conversation with Bud had shaken him more than he ever would have anticipated. Up until now he had been thinking of him as kind of a rebound guy—a nerdish type character whose sole function was to fill in some time for Julie and give her ammunition to use when her mother got on her case about the fact that she wasn't dating.

Now, suddenly, he saw him differently. Bud was quiet, but far from dull, with a seriousness and intensity that a sensitive girl like Julie could find appealing. Even the difference in their ages no longer seemed to Ray to be in his own favor. Bud might be three or four years older, but he was definitely not over-the-hill in any sense. He had the confidence of a man who knew what he wanted.

And apparently what he wanted was Julie. *Well, he's not going to get her,* Ray assured himself. *Not if I have anything to do with it.*

He walked back along the street to the spot where he had parked his father's car. He got into it and started the engine. He was so lost in his thoughts, he didn't notice another car that pulled into the lane behind him and followed him at a slight distance the whole way home.

CHAPTER 15

Helen had just started down to the pool when she heard the muffled sound of the telephone ringing inside her apartment.

"You go on down," she told Collie, who was walking beside her. "It might be about Barry."

She let herself back into the apartment and caught the phone on its sixth ring.

"Glad you answered. I was about ready to hang up." Ray's voice through the receiver sounded thin and far away. "I've got some good news for you. I saw Barry this afternoon, and he says the motive for the shooting was robbery. It didn't have anything to do with last summer. It was just some freak out to get cash."

"You saw Barry!" Helen's mind went no further than the

initial statement. "But, how could you? You're not a relative!"

"I didn't claim to be. I sneaked up the back stairs between visiting hours," Ray said. "Did you understand what I just told you about the shooting?"

"Yes, of course." Helen's hand tightened on the receiver. "How is he, Ray? How did he look? Did he mention me at all?"

"I didn't talk to him very long," Ray said. "He didn't look great, but who would the day after a bullet's dug out of his back? He was plenty lucid though. He knew what he was saying."

"Do you think I could get in to see him too?" Helen asked him. "If I went up the way you did?"

"Look, Helen, I wouldn't try it." There was an odd note in Ray's voice. "He's feeling pretty down right now and isn't exactly in the mood for visitors even if the doctors would permit it. You'd be wiser to wait until he's feeling better."

"But if he was glad to see you—" Helen began.

"He wasn't. And he wouldn't be to see you either. Believe me, Helen, I know what I'm talking about. He's depressed. Let him be for a while, okay?"

"Okay, Ray. Thanks for calling. Have you told Julie?"

"I haven't been able to get hold of her yet," Ray said. "But I'm trying."

"Well, thanks again," Helen told him. "It's good to know the rest of us don't have to worry about getting shot at."

She hung up the phone with a sigh of mingled relief and frustration.

The idea that Barry might not want to see her was, of course, ridiculous—too ridiculous even to argue about. If Barry was feeling depressed it was exactly the time when he needed to see her the most. There would be no sense in trying to go over to the hospital tonight when his parents were sure to be there, but she would certainly do so first thing in the morning.

As for the motive of robbery for the attack on Barry, well that settled once and for all the question of breaking the pact. She knew that as long as she lived she would never forgive Ray for making that suggestion. The fact that he would even consider going to the police without clearing the move with Barry first showed how little honor he had for an agreement.

Suppose he had done it, she thought now. *Suppose he had just gone ahead and done it without even talking to Barry! He would have ruined Barry's whole life for no reason at all.*

She had tossed her towel onto the chair beneath the wall phone. Now she picked it up and started back across the room to the door. She stepped through it, hesitated a moment, and then pulled it closed without locking it.

"Terror time's over," she said aloud.

The words had a good ring to them, and she realized suddenly, as she said them, that she had been frightened. Not frightened enough to agree to break the pact, but good and nervous. *Well, that part's over, thank god,* she thought as she walked along the balcony and down the steps to the pool.

Collie was standing by one of the deck chairs, chatting with the prettier of the two schoolteachers from Apartment 213. Actually, it was the girl who was doing the talking. Collie was giving her polite attention, but his eyes flicked immediately to Helen when she appeared on the stairs and did not leave her as she came across to join them.

"Hi," he said. "Important call?"

"A report on Barry. A friend of his crashed the guard and got in to see him this afternoon. He was phoning to tell me about him."

"How is poor Barry?" the schoolteacher asked. She gave Collie an innocent smile. "Barry Cox is Helen's boyfriend and a total hottie. It's no wonder she doesn't have eyes for anybody else, right, Helen?"

"Right," Helen said agreeably. "And he's better, thank you. He's going to be just fine."

"Good news," Collie said. "Come on. I'll race you the length of the pool."

He dove in ahead of her and, standing by the pool's edge, Helen watched him swim, using long, powerful strokes as though to work off a fit of anger.

The schoolteacher got up from her chair and came over to stand beside her.

"You're a glutton," she said, and the light little laugh that was supposed to take the venom from the statement was forced. "You're not playing fair."

Helen turned to her in surprise. "What are you talking about?"

"How many guys do you need, one for every day of the week?" The girl nodded toward Collie, who already had nearly completed the length of the pool. "You've got your beloved Barry. Leave something for the rest of us!"

"Oh, Collie's just a friend," Helen said.

"Does he know that?"

"Of course! He was the one who drove me down to the hospital the night Barry was shot. He knows all about him."

"I don't care what he knows," the girl said shortly. "He hasn't looked at anyone but you since the day he arrived. The rest of us girls haven't been able to get so much as a conversation going with him. He's polite enough, but he looks right through us as though his mind were somewhere else entirely. If you must know—" she laughed again, this time with real amusement, "I've gotten a lot more of a reaction from Barry than I have from this guy."

"Barry's nice to everybody," Helen said coolly. Turning her back upon the girl, she dove into the water.

The shock of the cold water jolted her into frenzied motion. Like Collie before her, she began to swim with fast, strong strokes to work off her fury. After a moment she felt calmer and turned onto her back to look at the girl behind her. She had turned away from the pool now and was returning to her deck chair.

Jealous, Helen thought, wrinkling her nose in distaste. She had accepted long ago the fact that she would have no real girlfriends at the Four Seasons. This knowledge did not particularly upset her, because she had never been a person to have girls as friends anyway. Even back in high school, the only person she had ever really considered a friend was Julie.

Even that had not been a friendship such as most girls had. Most of Julie's time had been tied up with clubs and cheerleading and other after-school activities. Their relationship had not been based so much upon their own personalities as upon the fact that the boys they dated hung out together.

Still, it had been Julie whom she had taken home with her to show off her prom dress, and it was to her that Elsa had blabbed the bit about the dress having come from a thrift shop. Julie had been gracious about that, and as far as Helen knew, she had never mentioned it to anyone. It was the sort of disclosure that the girls from Four Seasons would have leapt at like hungry wolves. She could hear it in her mind's ear, being jabbered up the line from apartment to apartment: "Do you know where Helen Rivers buys her dresses?"

Well, she didn't have to worry about that kind of thing any longer. Helen permitted herself a smile of satisfaction. Let the little bitches rake her over the coals just as long as the raking was inspired by jealousy. Nobody minded being considered too beautiful or too successful or too lucky. If those were the things they were going to pounce on, let them pounce. No matter what they said, they took vicarious pleasure in the fact that Channel Five's Future Star lived here among them, spilling some of the glamour of her own life over into their dull ones. Nobody could look at the way she dressed now and make any comments about trips to the thrift shop.

The move into the apartment had been the grandest event of her life. Even Elsa had been impressed and had shown it.

"How about our moving in together?" she had suggested in a rare moment of sisterly friendliness. "I could chip in for part of the rent, and we could take turns doing the cooking and stuff."

The suggestion was so preposterous that for a moment Helen had been too stunned to answer.

"Oh, no!" she had said at last. And then, seeing her mother's concerned face framed in the kitchen doorway, had added quickly, "I'm going to rent a one-bedroom. I'll be keeping all kinds of funny hours, and I'll need to sleep in the mornings. Besides, we can't both leave home at once. Who would be here to help Mom with the children?"

"Don't you worry, Elsa," their mother had said, coming into the room to put an arm around her older daughter's plump shoulders. "Helen will be right here in town. She can come home to see us whenever she wants to. And your time will come too. All little birds fly the nest."

The glitter of envy in her sister's eyes had filled Helen with a sense of half-guilty satisfaction.

"You couldn't afford it anyway, Elsa," she had said. "I'm going to take an apartment at the Four Seasons, and the rents there are astronomical."

And I did it, she thought now, beginning to move her arms in a slow backstroke. *I'm here, right where I said I'd be.*

The Four Seasons was the first apartment complex she had looked at, and the moment she had seen it, shining like some special fairyland with the pool, the bright beds of flowers, the wooden balconies, the gregarious crowd of moneyed, young singles who lived there, she had known that this was the culmination of her dreams.

"Barry will love it," she had told herself, and she had been right. The incredulous expression on his face the first time she had shown him into the blue and lavender apartment had been enough to erase any shadows cast by Elsa's cruel comments.

"So this is how a Future Star lives!" he had commented, and though the remark had been made half-teasingly, there had been a look of renewed interest in his eyes. Helen Rivers might not have social background or a lot of education, but she certainly wasn't a nothing.

Now she paddled leisurely to the end of the pool where Collie was waiting for her. He had pulled himself up onto the edge and was sitting there dripping, his brown hair plastered over his forehead.

He said, "You are without doubt the laziest swimmer I've ever seen."

"Well, it's a long pool."

She smiled up at him, knowing how well her wet hair framed the shape of her face. She knew too how she looked in the tiny, blue bikini—better than the schoolteacher at the far side of the pool and better by a long shot than any of the other girls who lived in the building. Of course, she was Barry's girlfriend, that was understood. But it didn't hurt anything at all to have somebody else admire her.

"You'll have to watch the news tonight," she said, "and see if I was able to get my hair dry."

"I won't be watching TV tonight." Collie's dark eyes regarded her without amusement. He made no effort to reach down and draw her up on the ledge beside him. "I'm going to be busy."

"Doing what?"

"I've got a date."

"You have?" She could not keep the surprise from her voice. "How could you? I mean, I didn't think you were seeing anybody."

"You thought I'd have fun eating my heart out while you mooned over your battered lover?" The words were light, but there was something in the tone that was not.

"No, of course not." Helen felt herself flushing with embarrassment. Hadn't that, actually, been exactly what she had thought? "What I meant was, I didn't know you had met anybody yet. After all, you just moved in here less than a week ago."

160

"There are other girls in the world besides the ones at Four Seasons," Collie told her. "This particular girl I'm seeing tonight is one I knew before I ever met you."

"Oh," Helen said awkwardly. "I didn't realize."

"You don't realize a lot of things," Collie said quietly. "You don't know what I do when I'm not with you, or where I come from, or what I'm interested in, or what I think about, or what courses I'm planning to take this summer. You don't know where I've worked, or how I live, or who the people are that I care about. You haven't been interested enough to ask. Everything we've ever talked about since the day we met has been you. And, of course, your wonderful Barry."

"I guess you're right," Helen said weakly. "But you don't have to make me sound so...so self-centered."

"You said it. I didn't."

There was no laughter in his face. Suddenly, Helen realized that she had almost never seen him laugh. Collie's face was dark and solemn, a face that had been places and seen things, perhaps some of them not very pleasant.

"You're a pretty girl," he said now. "I'll give you that. But there are plenty of people in the world besides you. You might try looking at them sometime. Some of them are interesting." He reached out and touched her chin with a blunt, strong forefinger.

"I'm interesting. Look at me sometimes. Ask me things. Listen to my answers. You just might find that I've got some

161

things to say that you would be interested in hearing. I may soon have a more important place in your life than you think right now."

Then, without waiting for her answer, he flipped himself onto his feet.

"So long," he said, just loudly enough for his voice to carry the length of the pool. "I'm off to get dressed for my date. She's a cute little redhead. Can't be late picking her up!"

I don't believe it, Helen thought. *I simply don't believe it!*

For a moment she remained there, stunned, gripping the side of the pool, as bewildered as if a pet puppy had suddenly planted its teeth in her wrist.

He's Collie, she thought. *My friend Collie! How can he possibly say things like that!*

Then she heard the laughter and turned to see that the schoolteacher in the deck chair had been joined by her roommate. Collie's farewell had been easily overheard, and they were enjoying it tremendously.

Slowly, Helen's astonishment began to be replaced by a rising wave of anger. *He did that on purpose*, she thought. *He was trying to embarrass me. Why that . . . that* bastard!

"You said it. I didn't." The words came back to her, and she clenched her teeth in fury. It was all she could do to keep from climbing out of the pool and racing up the stairs to intercept him on the balcony.

But she couldn't do that. It would look as though she were chasing him. She would have to swim a while longer and then sit around the pool for a time, chatting with people, as though Collie Wilson didn't mean a thing to her. Which, of course, he didn't.

In the meantime, who was this girl he had known before he met her? And just how well did he know her?

CHAPTER 16

Mrs. James put the last of the dinner dishes into the dishwasher and poured herself a final cup of coffee to carry with her into the living room.

It was a lovely evening. The windows stood open to the breeze, and spring poured into the house with the faint sweetness of the first hyacinths and the thin chirp of an early cricket.

It's beautiful, Mrs. James thought, seating herself on the sofa and placing the cup on the coffee table before her. *It's a heavenly night — things went well at school today — Julie's been accepted at Smith. By rights I should be floating on air. So why do I feel so strange?*

Because she did. It was an odd, prickly feeling along the back of her neck.

Something is going to happen, she thought. *I don't know what it will be or how I know it, but there is something in the air. Something bad is going to happen, and there is nothing I can do to prevent it.*

It was not the first time she had had such a feeling. Premonitions had come to her off and on throughout her adult life. The first time it had happened had been when Julie was only eight. It had been in the middle of the morning, a nice, normal morning with the sunlight pouring down golden into the yard and the chatter of birds in the elm tree. Mrs. James had been kneeling in the grass, pruning the roses, when suddenly she had stiffened with the realization that something was wrong.

Perhaps, she had thought, *I have left a stove burner on or forgotten an appointment. Is there a phone call I was supposed to return and have forgotten about? Is there an invitation I haven't answered? What in the world could it be?*

Chiding herself for her silliness, she had nevertheless gone back into the house to check the stove and her calendar, and while she was there the phone had rung. It was the school calling to say that Julie had fallen on the playground and broken her arm.

The next time the feeling had come to her it had been one year later. This time it had been so strong, so sharp, that it had been almost a physical pain.

"What is it?" she had cried aloud, and she had not been surprised a short time later to see a police car pull up in front of the house. She had gone to the door and stood there waiting as the two uniformed officers had come toward her across the lawn.

"Mrs. James?" one of them had said. "I have bad news for you, ma'am. There's been an accident. Your husband's car—"

"Yes," Mrs. James had said dully. "Yes, I know." She had gone to get her purse and had not seen the astonishment in the men's eyes.

In the years since her husband's death, the feelings had never occurred so strongly again. They had been there though, off and on, and almost always they had predicted trouble.

There had been the time the light switch had shorted, and the kitchen had caught fire. She had been at a PTA meeting, and had called Julie, who was visiting at a friend's house, and had said, "Run home and check on things, will you, dear? I have one of my feelings."

Julie had reached home in time to call the fire department, and the damage to the house had been minor.

Not that the feelings were foolproof and could be taken as gospel. Last summer, for instance, there had been a time when she could have sworn that she felt something terrible approaching. It was during a period in which Julie was seeing a great deal of Ray, and for a while Mrs. James had wondered if that was it, if the young people's feelings for each other were growing too strong and would create a problem. Fond as she was of Ray, she was aware of his immaturity, and she wanted another year of high school for Julie and then hopefully college. The idea of an unwed pregnancy or a very young marriage was not easy for her to accept.

In this case, however, the problem had not materialized. There had been one long evening when she had lain awake, counting the minutes, waiting for Julie and her friends to return from a cookout in the mountains. That night she had known that something would happen. Then, how silly she had felt when Julie had come home safely no later than midnight. Soon after that she and Ray had stopped seeing each other, and Ray had gone off to the West Coast.

Since then she had carried with her a strange, troubled feeling about Julie, but it was nothing that she could pinpoint. Her daughter had seemed different—quieter, more studious. Her social life had fallen away to almost nothing, but that might simply have been because Ray was gone.

"She's growing up," Mrs. James had told herself. "There's nothing especially wrong. She has just changed from a light-hearted little girl into a serious-minded young woman."

She was not sure that she completely favored the change. The old, happy-go-lucky Julie had been fun to live with. But then, she reminded herself, no mother really liked to see her child grow up.

This month, however, there had been something else. A growing restlessness. A nervousness within herself. She could not put her finger on the reason.

Something's not right, she had thought.

More and more often on the days on which she substituted and had to remain after hours to make notes for the regular teacher's return, she had called home to see that Julie was safely back from school and, if not, she had called her on her cell. She had all but stopped her own evening activities, the meetings and plays and card games which she often attended with her friends. She felt she should be at home.

"In case," she told herself, trying to laugh. In case of what, she did not know.

But tonight she did know. Tonight there was a reason. She had not been able to rid her mind all day of the picture of Julie as she had been the night before, standing in the kitchen, looking at her with pleading in her eyes. Pleading for what? What did she want or need?

"Mom," she had said. "Mom, I love you so much."

How long, how many years, had it been since she had burst out with something like that? It had been almost as though she were begging for something, asking for help.

"Mom," she might have said, "I need you!" It had been in the voice if not in the words.

Something is wrong, Mrs. James thought now, staring at the untouched cup of coffee on the table before her. *If I knew what it was, I could fight it, but I don't know. I can't even begin to imagine.*

Julie had gone to her room to dress for her date with Bud. The sound of her CD player flowed down the stairs and the music trickled into the living room, mingling with the scents and sounds of spring.

It was a beautiful night and, Mrs. James realized with growing apprehension, it was a night when something terrible was going to happen to somebody.

Mr. Rivers tilted his chair back against the kitchen wall and asked, "Are there any more potatoes?"

"Of course there are. If there's anything we've always got, it's potatoes." His wife wiped the back of her hand across her forehead and opened the oven to take out the bowl. "Elsa, don't you go digging into them, now. Dad needs to eat, and you don't need any extra helpings."

"You want me to look like Helen, is that it?" Elsa said irritably. "Well, you might as well forget it. I'm not about to starve myself like she does in hopes some TV station will offer me a contract."

"Helen's got willpower," Mr. Rivers said, helping himself to the gravy. "It's gotten her where she wants to go."

"And she hasn't cared who she walked over to get there."

Mrs. Rivers turned away from the oven. She was a thin, sallow-faced woman who for one brief time in her teens had been mildly pretty. Since then the advent of baby after baby, housework, ill-health, and the constant weight of financial problems had combined to give her a look of permanent exhaustion. The violet eyes, which had been her gift to her second daughter, looked oddly out of place in her drawn face.

"I don't like to hear you talk that way, Elsa," she said. "It sounds like you begrudge your sister a happy life."

169

"Well, I don't see where she deserves one," Elsa said with a burst of feeling. "It's not fair that she should have it all — looks, a cushy job, all kinds of money. What has she done to earn all that, I'd like to know? Helen's never had a thought for anyone but herself in her whole life."

"She helps out here," her father reminded her. "She sends a check every payday."

"Not as much as she could. Not so much that she can't buy anything she wants for herself. She's selfish, Dad, and you know it, but you'll never admit it. Helen's always been your favorite."

"Dad doesn't have favorites among his children," Mrs. Rivers told her, "any more than I do. We love all of you just alike, and we're glad for anything good that happens to any one of you. You'll have your chance, Elsa. Your luck'll turn. You'll meet some nice boy."

"Like Barry Cox?"

"Maybe. Who knows who you'll meet."

"I know," Elsa said bitterly. "It'll never be anybody handsome and rich like that. It'll be somebody who's a nothing, and I'll marry him because nobody else asks me, and we'll live in a house like this one and have a million kids just like you did. And we'll live on mashed potatoes."

"Talking about kids," her father said shortly, "go look in on 'em, will you? It sounds like they're tearing the living room apart."

"I'm glad Helen's boyfriend got hurt," Elsa said. "Maybe

this will show her she can't have everything perfect."

She got up from the table and left the room. Her voice floated back to her parents, "What do you kids think you're doing? Get those trucks off that sofa!"

Her mother shook her head. "What did we do wrong?"

"We didn't do anything wrong," Mr. Rivers told her. "We did the best we could, all things considered. Like you said, there'll be a life for Elsa if she gets out and looks for it and stops using her sister for an excuse not to."

"But she's right in a way," Mrs. Rivers said softly. "Helen is selfish. And she does seem to have everything."

"No, she doesn't," her husband said softly. "Not nearly. When she finds somebody to love her, then maybe she'll have everything. But the way she's going, that'll take a long time. First she'll have to learn to think past herself to somebody else."

"But she's so pretty," Mrs. Rivers objected. "There's not a man in this world who wouldn't want Helen. Just look at the Cox boy!"

"I didn't say 'want' her," Mr. Rivers said gently. "I said 'love' her. And about her looks—" He got up from his chair and put his hands on his wife's stooped shoulders. "I'll tell you one thing, honey; Helen may be pretty compared to some girls, but she'll never hold a candle to her mother."

"Do you think he knows?" Mrs. Cox asked nervously. "Do you think Barry guesses that he isn't going to walk again?"

"Why do you say something like that?" Mr. Cox asked her. "The doctor told us that isn't definite. There's still hope."

"But he said if a week passed and there wasn't some sign of movement in his legs—"

"A week hasn't passed. This is only the end of the second day."

They had just stepped from the elevator into the hospital corridor. Evening visiting hours had begun, and friends and relatives of patients, many of them laden with books and flowers, moved past them in hurried little groups.

Mr. Cox turned to regard his wife with a kind of despair.

"Sometimes, Celia, I almost think you're wishing this fate on Barry. You're so glad to get him firmly anchored under your thumb that you don't even mind the fact that he might be restricted to a wheelchair."

"What a dreadful thing to say!" Mrs. Cox was sincerely shocked. "Of course I mind! This is a horrible thing to have happened to Barry! Still, I don't begrudge a minute of the time I'll be spending taking care of him. He's my son, my own baby. I'll do everything I can to make life pleasant for him when he comes home."

"Face it, Celia," Mr. Cox said quietly, "you've done your best to run that boy's life for him since the day he was born. You couldn't stand the thought that any part of it might be something that didn't include you. No wonder he started rebelling during his last year of high school, picked up a girl you didn't approve of, started smoking pot and driving like a madman. A boy needs some breathing room if he's ever going to grow into a man."

"He's had all the breathing room he could possibly want," Mrs. Cox said angrily. "We're sending him to college, he's been living at a fraternity house—"

"He's here at the University because you didn't want him moving out of town. And the fraternity house is something you gave in on to keep him from taking an apartment somewhere else."

"If you're accusing me of not loving Barry—"

"I'm not accusing you of that." Mr. Cox reached out with an unaccustomed gesture and took both her hands in his. "I'm not saying it's all been your fault either. If I'd been home more, if I hadn't been so wrapped up in my work, you wouldn't have had to center your life on Barry. What I am saying is that we've got to face the situation and do something about it. When Barry leaves the hospital, he'll have to come home with us, yes. But not to stay. If the worst comes true, if our son never walks again, he is not going to spend the rest of his life with us."

"What are you saying?" she gasped. "How can you possibly suggest that we just throw our crippled child out on the street!"

"You know perfectly well that's not my meaning. Just because a man can't walk doesn't mean he's destined to be a helpless invalid. Barry can continue college, graduate, and go into some line of work that he can handle from a desk. He can drive a car with hand controls. He can support himself, live where he likes, travel without us. What I'm saying is that we're going to give him a chance to grow up."

Releasing her hands, he turned abruptly and started down the hall. After a startled moment, Mrs. Cox hurried to catch up with him.

"But that girl," she exclaimed, "that Rivers girl, what are we going to do about her? In the weakened state Barry's in, somebody will have to protect him from opportunists. What if he should decide—"

"Mr. and Mrs. Cox?" As they drew opposite Barry's room, the white-haired doctor was just coming through the doorway. He pushed the door closed behind him. "I have some happy news for you."

His lined face looked unaccountably younger than it had that morning.

"Your son just moved his left foot."

"He did?" Mr. Cox stopped so suddenly that his wife bumped into him from behind. "He moved his foot? Then that means—"

"It means that we're on the road up," the doctor said warmly. "It'll take time, of course, and extensive therapy, and I can't guarantee that he's going to be back on the football field any time soon. But if Barry can move his foot, he's going to be able to move his legs. And if he can do that, he'll walk."

"Thank god!" Mr. Cox let out a long breath of relief. "Do you hear that, Celia?"

"Yes," his wife said softly. "Oh yes!" She reached for the

knob of the closed door. "Oh, I can't wait to see him!"

"I'm afraid you'll have to," the doctor told her. "Barry has asked that he be given some time without visitors."

"But we're not visitors!" Mrs. Cox objected. "We're his parents!"

"He asked for the telephone," the doctor said, "and he's making a call. It's odd the way these emotional jolts affect people. The first thing he said when he realized the significance of what was happening, seeing his foot move under the sheet, was 'I've done a terrible thing.'"

"A terrible thing?" Mrs. Cox repeated. "Why, Barry's never done wrong to anybody in his life. What could he be thinking of?"

"He said he lied to somebody," the doctor said. "It was all pretty confused. You know, he's been under sedation and he's still a bit groggy. He said he'd lied to somebody, and he had to straighten it out before it was too late."

"I don't understand," Mr. Cox said, frowning. "He hasn't seen anybody but us since the accident. Whom could he have lied to? And about what? You'd better let me talk to him."

"I'm sorry," the doctor said firmly, "but he's making a phone call and he was very definite about wanting to make it in private."

The telephone began to ring in Helen's apartment. It rang twelve times before it stopped.

The man in the low-seated lavender chair sat quietly until

it had finished. Then he flexed his strong hands and laid them flat on his knees. There was a smear of yellow paint across the back of one of them.

He had come in easily, for the door to the balcony had not been locked. Now there was nothing for him to do except wait.

CHAPTER 17

Helen could hear the telephone ringing as she climbed the steps and hurried along the terrace toward her apartment. She had stayed at the pool much longer than she had intended.

Collie's abrupt departure had been noted not only by the schoolteachers, but also by everyone else within earshot. So, swallowing her anger, Helen had swum back and forth a while longer and then climbed out of the water to join the progressively larger crowd of young people who were gathered around the pool to enjoy a period of after-work relaxation. She had accepted a beer, something she seldom indulged in, from the lawyer in Apartment 107, and had laughed and chatted with such vivacity that she was soon surrounded by a circle of masculine admirers. Even after the schoolteachers had given up and gone to their apartments for dinner, Helen had remained, sipping and talking and watching the evening settle.

When the gaslights around the pool went on, she glanced across at the lawyer's watch.

"I've got to get changed," she said, "and get down to the studio."

"Why change?" the lawyer asked jovially. "You'd be a hit as is!"

But Helen had gotten to her feet, laughing, tossed the empty beer can into his lap, and circled the pool to mount the stairs. She could hear the muffled sound of the phone when she reached the second balcony, and she quickened her footsteps. The apartment door was unlocked, so this did not detain her. Nevertheless, the moment her hand touched the receiver, the phone stopped ringing.

"It's making a habit of that lately," Helen said aloud. "Well, maybe whoever it is will phone back. Or maybe it was Elsa and I'm lucky to have missed her."

"Do you usually leave your apartment open?" a voice asked her.

The voice, so unexpected, was like a cold hand on her neck. Helen whirled in panic and then, with a gasp of relief, felt all the defense drain out of her as she saw the man in the purple arm chair.

"Oh Collie! You scared me to death. What are you doing here?"

"Waiting for you." He had changed out of his trunks and

was neatly dressed in a polo shirt and trousers. His hair, still wet from the pool, was slicked down across his forehead. "You took your time about coming up. I thought maybe something had happened to you."

"I was having a good time down there," Helen said defiantly. She crossed the room and turned on the light at the far end of the sofa. "I thought you said you had a date tonight. Did you decide not to keep it?"

"There's plenty of time for that," Collie said. "My date's not till eight. I thought maybe I'd better explain to you what I'm going to do on my date and who it's with."

"You don't have to do that," Helen told him. "I don't have any strings attached to you. You're free to date anybody you want to."

"True," Collie said. He got to his feet and pulled his chair around so that it blocked the doorway. "Sit down, Helen. Over there on the sofa. Now, about my date—"

"I told you," Helen said, "that it doesn't matter."

"Don't interrupt. I know what you told me. The thing is that I'm going to do something interesting to my date tonight. I'm going to kill her."

"You-you're going to do what?" She knew that she could not have heard him correctly, but the words had been so clear. She stared at him blankly. "You're making a joke, and I don't think it's funny."

"It's not funny at all." Collie's face was set and expressionless. "Killing people is never funny, whether you do it with a gun or a grenade or a bomb or with your bare hands. If you run somebody down with a car, a little kid on a bike going home to his mother, that's not funny, either. Not for the kid. Not for his family."

"B-but, how did you know? Who told you about that?" The question caught on her tongue and threatened to strangle her.

"Nobody told me. I had to do a lot of searching to find it out. They didn't tell me when Danny was killed. They couldn't reach me with the news. I was in Iraq, waiting to be flown back here to a hospital. By the time I got the message it was all over—the funeral—everything. I never got home for it."

"Who are you?" Helen whispered. "Who the hell are you?"

"You know that. I'm Collingsworth Wilson. My mother is married to a man named Michael Gregg. Danny Gregg was my half brother."

"Your half brother!" Helen repeated shakily. "Oh, my god!" Collie did not seem to hear her: His eyes were dark with remembering.

"All I could learn when I finally did get home was what my folks could tell me. They said it was a hit-and-run, and the person who called the police had sounded like a teenager. He had said, 'We hit him,' so there was more than one person in the car. There were a lot of people at the funeral, my step-dad said. He showed me all the cards and the sympathy letters. He said there was a whole raft of yellow roses that came without a card. They were delivered from People's Flower Shoppe."

"I went down to People's and talked to the saleswoman. She remembered the roses. She said they'd stuck in her mind because it was so odd to see a young girl come in and spend so much money for flowers and then not put a name on the card. The girl had red hair and was wearing a silver cheerleading megaphone on a chain around her neck."

"Julie," Helen murmured. She knew that she should be running, screaming, doing something, but she was too numb for movement. Her throat muscles did not work. Her mouth formed the name, "Julie."

"It took me a while to find her. First I went around to the different high schools during the basketball games, but there weren't any cheerleaders who were redheads. Then I started asking about last year's cheerleaders. I got talking with some of the guys in the bleachers at halftime, and pretty soon one of them mentioned this cute girl with red hair who had dropped off the squad. Just wasn't interested any longer—she had gone intellectual and dropped out of everything. Wasn't even dating."

"But you couldn't have known," Helen said. "You couldn't have been sure."

"I wasn't at first, but it gave me an idea. I decided to send her a note through the mail, something that would shake her up if she was the right person but wouldn't mean a thing to her if she wasn't. She reacted, all right. That very afternoon she was over here like a shot, and so was your friend, Barry. That's how I learned about you, and I followed Barry when he left that night. I watched him walk into the frat house. I learned where he lived that way."

"And that's when you moved into Four Seasons?" Helen's shock was fading and she was beginning to come alive again. Her eyes shifted slightly, judging the distance from the sofa to the door. Collie's chair sat directly in the path. The window was closed. If she could reach it and yank it open and scream—

"You'll never make it," Collie said, reading her thoughts. "I'm closer than you are, and you'd never have time to pull it open. Don't you want to hear the rest?"

"No," Helen said with mounting terror. "I don't."

"Well, you're going to, so you'd better relax and listen. Yes, I moved in here at Four Seasons, and I met you, and you filled me in on Barry. You said you'd gone with him all last year, so I knew he had to have been the one with you that night. I gave him a test too. I phoned him and gave him a story about having some pictures of the accident. He said he'd meet me out on the athletic field to look at them."

"And you shot him? You?"

"Right."

"But, why?" Helen asked in horror. "Why would you do such a thing? I can understand how you would feel about your brother and how you'd want to see us punished. But couldn't you just have gone to the police?"

"How would I have proved it?" Collie asked her.

"You wouldn't have had to. Just being accused would have been enough. We would have confessed."

182

"And what do you think would have happened to you once you did? You'd have been fined, perhaps. Whoever was driving would have had his license revoked. Maybe the driver would have spent a little time in jail with his sentence reduced by half for good behavior. The law is easy on minors. Whatever happened, it wouldn't have been enough. Look at it through somebody else's eyes for a change. Look at it through my eyes."

I don't want to see anything through his eyes, Helen thought in terror. *I don't even want to look at his eyes. There's something wrong with them. They're getting darker! All the time he's been talking, they've been getting darker and darker. How could I ever have thought he had nice eyes?*

"Listen, Helen," Collie continued in his low, matter-of-fact voice, which was somehow more dreadful than a voice with emotion. "I cracked up over in Iraq; did I tell you that? Not just me but plenty of other guys too. There's something about seeing people blown to pieces that kind of gets to you. So, I come home from Iraq, and what do I find? My kid brother dead. My mother in a loony bin in Las Lunas. My stepdad down there with her. My sister Meg living all by herself in the house in the mountains, worrying herself sick about everybody. Our whole family is wrecked, and what about you four, the ones responsible? One of you has a plush job in TV. One is a college football hero. One's off lolling on California beaches, and one's just been accepted at Smith. All your lives are going along just great."

"So, you decided to kill us." Helen spoke the words, but she could not bring herself to believe them.

This is Collie, she thought. *The guy who lives two apartments over and has a slight crush on me. This is the kind person who came to pick me up at the studio the night Barry was shot. He drove me to the hospital and waited there with me until there was news. Why did he do that? Why was he so good to me?*

"I took you to St. Joseph's," Collie said in answer to the unspoken question, "because it was the only way I had of learning what had happened to the bastard. It was dark out there on the field, and he jumped when the flashlight went on. I wasn't sure where I hit him. I meant to do the job right, but the way it turned out, this might be even better. For a guy like Barry, life in a wheelchair could be worse than no life at all."

Helen's cell phone, which was on a side table plugged into a charger, rang sharply. The sound was sudden, jabbing through the tension in the room like a needle, causing Collie to jerk upright in his chair and shift his eyes for an instant away from Helen's face.

In that instant, she moved. As the cord of terror that had been holding her in place was suddenly broken, Helen was on her feet, bolting across the room. She did not try to reach the door or the window. Instead she whirled and ran in the opposite direction, through the bedroom, into the bathroom.

Slamming the door behind her, she punched the lock just seconds before the bulk of Collie's weight struck the door.

The knob rattled angrily. Frantically, Helen glanced around

for something to arm herself with. All around her, flimsy, feminine objects mocked her—a makeup kit, a plastic hairbrush, a rack of fluffy bath towels, a small bottle of bubble bath.

The bathroom window was small and high, plated over with a permanent sheet of translucent glass.

The rattling of the knob stopped abruptly. The only sound now was the continued ring of the phone in the front room. Then that stopped also.

"Collie?" Helen said nervously.

There was no answer other than a heavy silence.

Less than two hours ago Ray had informed her that the attack on Barry had been simple robbery. How could Barry have lied to them that way, lulling them into a false sense of security? Or was it Ray who had been lying?

"It couldn't have been Ray," Julie had said on that day—was it really only a week ago when she had brought the note that Collie had sent her over to this very apartment? "I know Ray better than either of you, and he just wouldn't do this."

"I don't think so either," Helen had agreed.

And now, in this new set of circumstances, she had to admit the same thing, silently, to herself, as she stood trembling behind the ominous silence of the locked door. Ray would not have tricked her. Ray would not have lied.

Ray had been repeating exactly what Barry had told him. "It was Barry," she said softly. "It was Barry who didn't tell the truth."

A hundred pictures of Barry flashed through her mind: Barry of the loving words and the cocky grin, of the flaring temper and the heavenly kisses. Barry who was going to marry her—or was he? Who adored her—or did he? Who had never looked at another girl—or had he? Ever since that day when he had drawn up behind her in that little red sports car and asked, "Do you want a ride?"

He lied, Helen thought. *He lied to Ray about the shooting!*

Why, she did not know, nor did it matter. Whether from anger over some imagined affront, from bitterness over his own injury, from perversity, from fear that Ray might break the pact and go to the police with the story of the accident, Barry had lied. And with this lie he had shown how little their safety meant to him—Ray's, Julie's, and Helen's.

"He loved me," Helen whispered, but even to her own ears the words were weak and meaningless. That was a lie too.

"Collie?" She spoke aloud. "Collie, are you out there?" There was nothing but silence on the far side of the door.

What was he doing? she asked herself. Standing there, waiting? Or was he back in the purple chair, sitting quietly, hoping that she would assume he had gone away, that she would open the door and step tentatively out? Could he possibly think she was that much of a fool?

If he wants me, Helen thought, *why doesn't he force the door?* He's strong enough. Of course, that would make a lot of noise, the kind of noise that carries. The whole apartment would shake. People would come running up here to see what was happening.

Screams would get her nowhere. The Four Seasons Apartments were virtually soundproof. Stereos could blare, televisions blast, wild parties churn until all hours of the night without disturbing the slumbering neighbors. But the sound of a door being beaten in — surely that sort of sound would make itself heard.

From the other side of the door there came a click. A faint, scraping sound of metal against metal.

What in the world—?

The noise came again. Faint. Purposeful.

Helen's eyes flew upward to the top of the door, and she felt her breath stop. The metal plate was moving.

"My god," she breathed, "he's taking off the hinges!"

I can't just stand here and wait for him to do it, she thought. *I have to do something — anything....*

Frantically, she yanked open the medicine cabinet over the sink and saw a heavy, glass bottle of perfume. Snatching it from the shelf, she stepped onto the closed toilet lid and then onto the top of the tank.

She lifted the bottle high and brought it down with all her strength against the pane of the window. Again and again she struck, smashing away the jagged glass.

There was no time to feel the pain, no time to consider the consequences as she thrust her head and shoulders through the narrow opening.

"Help!" she cried. "Somebody help me! Help me!"

Voices floated up from the pool area at the side of the building — laughter, the twang of a guitar. The lawn below her lay empty. The glow of the gaslights was broken by pockets of darkness.

"Help!" Helen screamed.

And then, because it was the only thing left to do, she wriggled forward through the frame of the window and let herself fall.

CHAPTER 18

"I wish you'd reconsider and stay home tonight." Mrs. James regarded her daughter worriedly. "It sounds silly, I know, but I have this feeling...."

"Oh, Mom! You and your feelings!" Julie spoke the words laughingly, but she could not completely obliterate the twist of uneasiness that stirred within her. There was something oddly disturbing about her mother's premonitions. Many times, it was true, they turned out not to mean a thing, but there had been other times also. It was hard to forget the phone call that had seemed so ridiculous, but had sent her home to find a smoke-filled kitchen.

"I'm just going out for a couple of hours," she said now, reassuringly. "It's just to a movie with Bud."

"I wish you'd call it off."

"Mom, I can't reach him. He's just moved into an apartment. The phone hasn't been installed yet and I don't have his cell number."

"Didn't you tell me he lives in Four Seasons?" Mrs. James persisted. "You could call there and leave a message for him at the office. Or you could phone Helen Rivers and ask her to run over to his apartment and tell him. I'm sure she wouldn't mind doing it. Everybody in those big complexes seems to know everybody else."

"It's probably too late. He's sure to have left by now." To humor her mother, Julie got up and went over to the telephone. She lifted the receiver, listened a moment, and set it down again. "I can't call anyway. There's trouble with the line again. There isn't even a dial tone. And I left my cell in Ray's car."

The framed mirror over the telephone table gave her face back to her, pinched and odd-looking under the flame of red hair. She raised her hand and pushed the hair back from her forehead.

I should have washed it, she thought. *I should have put on blush, my face looks so pale. What am I doing, going out on a date, looking like this? What is Bud going to think of me?* Not that it mattered. Bud was just Bud—he could think what he chose. If he didn't ask her out again, that was all right too. When she thought back upon last year, on the hours she had spent getting ready to go out with Ray—hair always clean and wavy, makeup perfect, heart filled with excited anticipation—it

190

was like looking back at another girl in another world.

Sometimes she wondered how she had ever started dating Bud in the first place. If their meeting had not been so simple, she probably wouldn't have. But he had just come over to her at the library and gestured to the book she was selecting and said, "You'll like that one. Let me show you another by the same writer that's even better." They had left the library at the same time, and it had seemed natural that he would fall into step beside her since they were headed in the same direction.

After that, date had followed date, because it had been easier to say yes than no. It had been a distraction, and it had gotten her through the long evenings. She had even tried to convince herself that she might come to care for Bud if she just kept seeing him long enough.

That was before Ray had come back. Fight it though she would, it had taken all of one instant, one glimpse of the quizzical green eyes, the thin face now bearded but warm and familiar, the merest touch of a hand, and she was back exactly where she had been in the beginning, when she had looked at this boy whom other girls hardly noticed and told herself, "This is the one."

And it wasn't fair, not to Bud, not to any of them. She should not be leading him on with false hopes when she felt like this about someone else.

The doorbell rang.

"That's Bud now," Julie said, and as she turned toward the door she caught a glimpse of her mother's face and stopped.

191

"Okay, Mom," she said softly. "I won't go."

"I know I'm being silly but—"

"That's okay. I don't really want to go anyway. I was just being stubborn." She went to the door and opened it. "Hi, Bud."

"Hello, Julie." He looked past her into the living room. "Hello, Mrs. James. How are you tonight?"

"Fine, thank you, Bud," Julie's mother said. "Come in and have a piece of cake with us, won't you? The coffee's fresh in the kitchen."

"I've decided I'd rather not see a movie tonight," Julie said apologetically, "if you don't mind too much, that is. Mom is sort of uptight and not feeling too great, and I'd kind of like to stay around home. Would it be okay with you if we just watched TV or something?"

"But it's a good film," Bud said. "I thought we'd agreed on it."

"Can't we see it another night?" Julie asked him. "It's going to keep playing all week."

"You promised you'd go tonight," Bud said.

His voice was flat and demanding. *How funny,* Julie thought in surprise, *I've never seen him act impatient before.*

Bud's face was set with a look of intensity. His eyes seemed very dark. There was something, some trick of light and shadow from the rays of the living room lamp filtering out as they reached him in the doorway, that made him for a moment look almost like a stranger.

I'm glad Mom made me promise not to go, Julie realized suddenly. *I don't want to go. I don't think I want to see this guy anymore at all.*

"If you're so hung up on seeing the movie tonight, why don't you go ahead without me?" she suggested.

"Look, Julie, we've got a date. You're not trying to dump me, are you, because your old boyfriend's back in town?"

"Oh, is that what this is about?" Abruptly the situation became clear to her. "Ray doesn't have anything to do with this, Bud, honestly. I just want to stay home tonight, that's all. You're welcome to hang out here or go on to the show on your own, whichever you want."

Bud stood silent a moment. His eyes flicked past Julie's face to her mother, then back again. He seemed to be considering.

"Okay," he said finally. "I recognize a brush-off when I'm getting one. How about walking me out to the car?"

Julie hesitated. She too wanted to turn and look at her mother, to consult with her in a glance, but to do so would have been actively rude.

This is crazy, she told herself firmly. *This is just Bud Wilson, just good old Collingsworth Wilson, and I've been out with him over a dozen times. What am I getting so jittery about tonight?*

"Look, I need to tell you something," Bud said. "It's important. Just walk out with me, okay?" He paused and then added, "I had lunch with him today. With Ray Bronson."

"You did?" She was startled.

"We did some talking, he and I."

"About me?"

"Among other things. Are you walking me out to the car, or aren't you?"

"All right," Julie said.

He held the door open for her, and she stepped out onto the front porch. They went down the steps together. The night air lapped around them, soft and sweet, and overhead the sky seemed to curve like a dark bowl, studded with stars.

"It's a pretty night," he said, and he reached over to take her hand. Julie felt a shudder run through her.

What's wrong with me? she asked herself in bewilderment. *Bud's held my hand before. It doesn't mean anything. I've never minded it. Why am I reacting like this now?*

She thought some of her Mom's funny feelings must be rubbing off on her.

But she didn't want to hurt him by drawing her hand away, so she let it lie in his as they walked across the yard to his car.

"Get in for a minute," Bud said. "Let's sit and talk."

"We can talk out here."

"What I want to say needs to be said with you sitting down," Bud insisted. "Get into the car, will you? It'll just take a minute."

"Bud—" Julie brought out the words in a burst, "whatever it is that you're going to tell me, I don't think it's something I should hear. You were right in what you said just now about

194

Ray. Whatever he told you when you saw him today is true. We used to matter to each other very much at one time and—and that feeling hasn't gone away. I hoped it would, but it hasn't. I don't think you and I ought to see each other anymore."

"Funny," Bud said, ignoring her statement. "You've never called me Collie."

"Collie?" She could not see his face in the darkness, but she was very much aware of his hand tightening on hers. "I didn't know you wanted me to. When we first met you told me that everybody in your family called you Bud."

"My kid brother started it." He spoke quietly. "Danny was a cute little kid. He couldn't say 'Collingsworth.' He called me Bubba—you know, for 'brother.' That was when he was a little guy. When he got older he changed it to Bud. He called our sister 'Sissy.'"

"That's—that's cute," Julie said uncomfortably.

What is he talking about? she asked herself in confusion. *He's acting so odd. I wonder if he's sick. I wonder if he's been taking drugs or drinking or something.*

She said, "I have to go in now. Mom isn't feeling well. Honest."

"My mother isn't either," Bud said. "She's in a lot worse condition than your mother. I have an account to settle with the four of you, but it hasn't all worked out as I planned it. You're the most important one, though. You're the one who made a joke of it by sending the flowers."

195

"Flowers?" Julie whispered. "You mean—oh, no! You're not—"

He released her hand. For a frozen instant Julie stood rooted, gathering herself to scream. Then the strong hands were around her throat and the scream started and ended in one short moan.

"Roses," Bud said. "Yellow roses—tons of them! Pa described them to me, all those roses that looked like sunshine! If you'd wanted to give him sunshine, why didn't you go back to him? Why didn't you sit in the road with him and hold his hand and wait with him? Did you really think you could buy us off with roses? What good are roses to a little boy who is dying alone in the dark?"

The hands were squeezing. There was nothing in the world now except those hands—the hands and the pain and the roaring in her ears and a million lights flashing behind her eyes.

He's going to kill me, Julie thought incredulously. *He's going to kill me!* It was impossible, the thing that the hands were going to do.

I don't want to die, Julie thought frantically. *I'm not ready to die. I haven't even lived yet. There's so much still ahead—college and work and a husband and children, my own home...so much living still ahead for me!*

What will this do to Mom? First Daddy and then me. She can't lose everybody!

I'll never see Ray again.

196

There was a time when she had looked into those tilted green eyes and said, "I love you."

So long ago. *He'll never know,* she thought wildly. *He'll never know that I still do!*

And then she was thinking no longer. The heavy blackness was all around her. And she knew at last what it was like to be alone in the night.

"Julie! Come out of it, Julie!" From a long way off the voice came down to her. Muffled and almost lost in the pounding of the blood through her head, the words came trickling through.

"Julie! Come back to us, Julie!"

It's a dream, she thought. *Do you dream when you're dead, I wonder? Is Danny Gregg dreaming? Is my father dreaming?*

"She's coming out of it," the voice said. It was familiar. It was not a dream voice. "Julie?"

She opened her eyes. The stars were so low that they seemed to be resting against her face. The porch light was on, and its dim yellow rays illuminated the features of the boy who bent over her.

"Julie, can you speak to us?"

"Ray?" She whispered his name, and the effort sent a thrust of agony through her throat. "Bud—he was going to—"

"I know," Ray said. His hand was on her hair, pushing it back from her face. "You don't have to worry. He's not going to be doing anything much for a while. I clobbered him with a flashlight from behind. It's not the way the good guys do it on television, but there wasn't time to think about that."

"Are you all right, darling?" Her mother was there also, kneeling on the ground beside her. "That boy must be crazy to attack you like that for no reason!"

"He had a reason," Julie told her. "And it was a good one. Ray, how did you know to come? How could you have guessed?"

"I didn't guess," Ray said. "Barry called me a few minutes ago. He said he was releasing us all from the pact, that we were in danger, all three of us, and to get hold of you and Helen. I tried calling her, but there wasn't an answer, and when I called you the line was out of order. Then I remembered something. It just flashed through my mind."

"What?" Julie asked him.

"Bud's hands. I sat with him today while he ate lunch, and he had paint on the back of one of his hands. It didn't register then, but after I talked to Barry it hit me. It was yellow paint—the same shade as the trim around the Greggs' roof. Remember, I wondered then how somebody as short as Megan could have reached it?"

"And the shirts on the line?"

"They were Bud's, of course. Megan's his sister."

"Please, tell me what this is all about," Mrs. James said in bewilderment. "I don't understand this at all. Did you come here tonight, Ray, knowing that Bud was going to try to harm Julie? If so, how—" She broke off the question. "What's this?"

Headlights cut the darkness of the street, and a car with a flashing red signal light pulled up to the curb in front of the house.

The car doors opened and slammed shut, and two uniformed figures hurried up the driveway.

"There was a 911 call," the first of the patrolmen said as he reached them. "The caller said you people might be having some trouble. A girl fell from a second-floor window at Four Seasons Apartments. She was knocked unconscious in the fall, but when she came to, she told the people who found her that a man named Wilson had tried to attack her. She thought he would be headed over here. From the looks of things—" His eyes took in the three of them and then shifted past them to the inert form that was lying on the ground a short distance away—"she was right."

"She was," Ray said. "There has been trouble, and it didn't just happen tonight. We want to tell you about it, from the very beginning."

He slid his arm under Julie's head and lifted her gently to a sitting position. Leaning against him, she looked across at her mother's worried face.

We can never erase it, she thought. *What we did last summer is done. We can't undo it, ever. But we can face it. That will be something.*

Aloud she said, "Why not you, Ray? You were involved as

much as the rest of us. Why is it that Bud never tried to do anything to you?"

"He did," Ray said softly. "Tonight." His arm tightened around her. "He knew the worst punishment for me would be to stay alive in a world that didn't have you in it."

Q&A WITH THE AUTHOR

Young adult author Barry Lyga sat down with

Lois Duncan to ask her all about

I KNOW WHAT
YOU DID LAST SUMMER

Barry: I KNOW WHAT YOU DID LAST SUMMER is probably the book that is most familiar to so many people for many reasons—one of which is the movie. I know many of your readers have seen the movie version and wondered about the differences between the book and the movie. Would you like to talk about that a little bit, and maybe give some insight as to why the movie turned out so differently from the book?

Lois: I guess the answer to that is, it's just plain more commercial to have things happening as they did in the movie. The movie was a shock to me. For one thing, this book was written in 1973, and I had almost forgotten I'd written it, so it was very exciting to learn that it was going to be a major motion picture. I could hardly wait to see it.

I went to the theater, bought my ticket and popcorn, and found a seat. Then onto the screen came an insane fisherman carrying an ice hook. He wasn't in my book. I thought, *You know, this is a big complex; maybe I've walked into the wrong theater.* So I was preparing to leave and then, no, up from below rolled the words "I Know What You Did Last Summer," and I thought, *That is my book, but who is that man and what is he going to do with that ice hook?* Well, I soon found out. He was going to decapitate my characters. Their heads were flying off, and their blood was spurting, and everybody was screaming, and *I* was screaming. I was so horrified I couldn't even open my popcorn. It was quite a shocker.

Barry: So you had no idea going into the movie what they had done with it? You had no communication with the movie production people at all?

Lois: Oh no, no. They kept me as far away as possible. I think they were afraid of how I might react if I realized what my little masterpiece was going to turn into.

Barry: Was it the fact that it was a slasher movie, period, or the fact that it had changed so radically from the book that shocked you? Or maybe a combination of the two?

Lois: Well, both, because I had expected it to be my story, and it *wasn't*. It was my characters and my plot gimmick, but then it went in all directions. Even the double-identity twist, which was the crux of the story, had been omitted. Also, I was quite horrified by the sensationalized violence. Several years earlier my own teenage daughter, Kait, had been chased down in her car and shot to death, and I had seen, right in front of my eyes, what real violence is. To have people screaming and laughing about it did not go down well.

Barry: So it almost sounds like this really drove home for you the difference between suspense and outright horror.

Lois: Yes, it did. I don't consider myself a horror writer, and this was horror. As I said, if you've known it in real life, then seeing it portrayed like that on the screen is a travesty. So I was not happy with the movie, but I have to admit I was happy with the fact that the book had been made into a movie, because that made all my backlist suddenly very popular. It was like getting a rebirth, but in a very strange way.

Barry: It's very bittersweet in a way. I want to talk a little bit about the character of Helen. She seems like an interesting mix of insecurity and ambition; did you want readers to like her or to find her shallow?

Lois: I never think about how readers are going to find a character. I just try to create the character, and then readers can relate or not relate, and that's going to depend on the reader. In real life we relate to people whom we have something in common with or understand, and it's the same with characters in books. So you can't create a character and say, "This is a character everybody will like," because we like different things, and we relate to situations that reflect our own lives and past history. So people can feel about Helen any way they choose to. There she is—I made her.

Personally, I think that Helen is one of the more interesting characters in this book because of her background. Helen sees her mother and the life her mother is living, and she wants to get out of that. She does not want to be drawn into following in her mother's footsteps. Yet Helen does not have a lot to work with the way Julie does, as far as being intellectual and having finances to further her education. So Helen, very cleverly, zeroes in on what her strong points are and she makes them sharper. She concentrates on where she wants to go by using the weapons at hand. So she really is a strong character. Julie is not in that situation, and Julie is hit much more strongly with guilt than Helen.

Barry: Speaking of characters, with the four main characters in the book you've set up a set of opposites. You have what some people would consider a "good girl" and a "bad girl," a "good boy" and a "bad boy." Was that intentional? Were you looking for that dichotomy? And do you see them as "bad" or "good"?

Lois: I see very few people either in real life or in books as totally "bad" or "good." In life, there are a few who may be totally "bad" because of some psychological disorder, but we see them very seldom, thank goodness. What I try to do is present the main viewpoint character as someone the reader can relate to, because I want at least one person the reader can like. If you don't have that, then the story itself doesn't matter, because the reader doesn't care what happens to anybody in it. So, in this case, I did have Julie and Ray, who are the more likable of the characters, and it was my choice to have a male and a female, because it gives you a double readership.

Barry: I know that something else on your mind and the minds of most people when the book came out was the Vietnam War. And now, of course, we deal with the Iraq war and the Afghan war. What sort of parallels you see between the wars going on now and Vietnam, and what, if anything, has really changed?

Lois: Well, this presented an interesting situation. When I learned that I was going to update these books, I thought this particular one was going to be a hard book to deal with because I needed Barry to go out onto the athletics field where a war demonstration was going on so that the sound of the gunshot would be lost in the explosions of the demonstration. How was I going to do that since that war was way in the past? And then I suddenly realized we now had another war just like it. That no matter where we are in history, we're probably going to have a war, and all you have to do is change the name of the war and you've got the same story.

I see very few differences between then and now—these are unpopular wars that many people feel we should not be or should not have been involved in, and there have been demonstrations in both cases. Here it transferred automatically into another war, and that's pretty a horrible thing to think about—that maybe twenty years from now if the book is still in existence and is again updated there'll be another war that can be substituted.

Barry: Now, the book ends before we can learn what will happen to the main characters for covering up the hit-and-run, and I assume that was intentional on your part. You wanted to end the book there—and I don't want to ask you what you imagined happened afterward because I think that's something interesting for readers to imagine themselves—but I'm curious, what was your reason?

Lois: There's a natural cutoff point for every story, and I thought we reached it. It's when you know that Julie's going to survive and the questions have been answered as to why things happened. I felt the book came to closure there, and to go on spinning along for another few chapters, adding things on, would be an anticlimax to say the least.

I've done that with all my books. I've ended the story as soon after the climax as I could, because I've seen too many books written by authors who just don't know when to stop. They just keep going and going. I think maybe those authors were told that they had to have so many words in the manuscript and realized they were missing a couple of thousand so they kept filling up pages until they used up their wordage.

Barry: I want to talk just a little bit about the updating of the book and I want to pull out just a single example that really struck me. Helen's blue pantsuit from the original book becomes just blue pants and a blouse with a chunky, crystal necklace, and it was really amazing to me how completely that changed the image of her that I had in my mind. Not just physically. Not just what she looked like, but the way she carried herself. The way she spoke. The way she acted. And it's just amazing how a few words can completely change something like that. As a writer, what sort of scares me is that words are so easy to manipulate. But I'm wondering—what's it like to know that just by tweaking a detail here and there, your original intent can be changed so much?

Lois: It was an interesting process to go through. Back when that book was originally written in 1973, women of all ages were wearing these shiny, polyester pantsuits. I realized that today no eighteen-year-old girl would be seen dead wearing one of those, so I looked at what they were wearing on television—what the news girls were wearing—and I thought *OK, that's what Helen's going to wear.* So I just changed it a bit, although I left it the same color. Yes, it did make her different, but not that terribly different.

She's still the same person, but certainly we wouldn't have wanted her gliding into the studio in one of those tacky polyester things.

Barry: One thing I found very interesting had to do with a sort of gender politics. There's a point where the character Barry has been talking to Helen, and he doesn't want to be in a deep relationship with her, and he's brushing her off. The text reads, "It was the first response he could think of and even to his own ears the statement had sounded ridiculous. All married women worked, at least until they had babies. Would Helen expect to have children? Yes, she probably would. A screaming, puking infant as quickly as possible."

Now, I know in the original he tells her that he doesn't want his wife to work and immediately even he feels like an idiot for saying it. That sort of dogma is portrayed as very old-school, very anachronistic, even in 1973. So now it's been updated and replaced by this fear of being tied down with kids. Could you talk a little bit about perceived sex roles when you wrote the book in the 1970s and also now?

Lois: Well, back in the '70s I think the majority of the women were stay-at-home housewives and the women's movement was just coming into effect. It was much more logical to say, "No wife of mine will ever work." Today that sounds utterly ridiculous, because certainly the large majority of married women *do* work.

But the bottom line in both editions of this book is that Barry did not want to get married. He didn't want to be tied down. He didn't want to mess up the nice career that was probably lying ahead for him and all the fun he was planning to have before he settled down. He was lying to Helen. He was just grabbing at any excuse to avoid her demands, which I think many men would do today as well.

However, today young people have the option to simply live together and marriage is less of an issue. Back in the '70s that would have been impossible. Nobody would have ever conceived of living with someone they weren't married to. For that reason, that excuse sounded even more farfetched when I read it this time. So I clarified it for the readers by inserting some of Barry's true feelings. He did not want to be tied down, a young husband with screaming children at the age of twenty.

Barry: That certainly worked. Another thing that was updated was the language, by which I mean swearing. In the original book you used "damn" and "hell" here and there. The new edition has phrases like "pissed off" and "shitty" in it. How much did you think about language when you originally wrote the book? Obviously, the sky's the limit with young adult literature now, but at the time, how much did you think about it?

Lois: I was very careful of it, and I'm still very careful of it. You're caught in a bind here. Do you have your characters talk the way kids really talk? Or do you have them talk the way adults *want* them to talk? Parents are in a very strong position as far as getting books banned in schools.

I've had my books ripped out of school libraries and classrooms by censors. By that, I mean literally. In one instance, five men in business suits charged into an English teacher's classroom and tore copies of the book out of the hands of students, leaving the teacher in hysterics. I've had books get challenged and banned all over the place. To some parents, there's nothing worse than having what they consider a "bad word" in a book, even if their kids and their kids' friends use that word all the time. What writer wants to get strung up by the fingernails for using a word that wasn't absolutely necessary to use?

At the same time, you want your dialogue to be natural. I've found this a very difficult challenge at every stage of my career. This book was getting challenged back when I first wrote it because I had used the word "damn" in it. My best compromise has been to hit a medium mark. In this edition, I used a few words that sound a little crude, even to me, but that's the way kids do talk, especially when adults aren't around. The other thing is that teenage slang changes constantly. For books that live on and on, as we hope our young adult books will, through generation after generation, just one word of slang can date a book and make it sound old-fashioned.

Barry: Were you tempted at all to take this opportunity to fix anything other than the updating of references for the purpose of making the books more modern?

Lois: Yes, I could see some things that I wished I hadn't done. Now that I'm reading and updating the books, I'm reading the books back-to-back. So I'm reading a book that I wrote in the 1970s and comparing it to a book I wrote in the 1990s, and I realize that I have repeated certain wording that I had forgotten all about, because when you've written fifty books it's hard to remember exactly how you've described things.

I would say something in some lovely manner and twenty years later would say it in exactly the same lovely manner. I had "sunlight sparkling on water forming pagan coins of light" in two different books. Okay, so there were fifteen years in between the times I wrote the books. It's beautiful, beautiful imagery but, my goodness, what if the same people read one book and immediately read the next book? They won't have fifteen years in between. It'll seem like I'm just repeating myself. So I catch things like that and try to make sure they didn't happen too often.

Barry: Were there things you saw and told yourself, *No, hands off. Unless it's updating I'm not going to touch it?*

Lois: Oh, I changed everything I wanted to change. I grabbed this opportunity. I'm actually having a wonderful time with this updating. It's like getting a renewed chance at life. To be given the chance to give my characters cell phones and computers and digital cameras is like rebearing my own children and providing them with wings.

Barry: Your books have been very popular for a very long time. Why do you think young readers like suspense novels?

Lois: Today's young readers have become conditioned by television. They tend to have short attention spans and are used to switching channels if there's a lull in the action. Suspense novels come closer to fulfilling their expectations of instant entertainment than most other genres. In other types of novels there can be long stretches of time in which the reader just has to sit there and wade through descriptions of scenery and analyze situations, waiting for something to occur. But suspense novels have a lot of action and there's the constant question of what is going to happen next. That's what causes the reader to keep turning pages.

It's a gimmick that I have learned, and I think most writers of young adult books have learned, because of television. That's how television works. You have a dramatic scene right at the beginning of the show that hooks the viewer, and then, if you have to, you go into flashbacks to show what led up to it. That's what readers are used to now. And, I have to admit, I've gotten used to it myself. I'm obsessed by suspense novels.

Barry: I agree. Something else I think worked well was your sort of casual treatment of underage drinking and marijuana use. You don't make a big deal about it. It's just something the kids are doing. At the time that the books were originally published, how was that received?

Lois: It was received very badly by a number of people who thought that if you mention something in a book, you're encouraging young people to do it. I would never want to encourage young people to do drugs or to drink, but they're doing it anyway, and it's very hard to write a contemporary book that ignores that fact. I could not very well have my kids going to a party where the parents are out of town and throw this big bash and have them all sitting around drinking soda pop and playing charades. It's just...I couldn't! It wouldn't be realistic.

Barry Lyga is the author of several acclaimed young adult novels including *Bang*, *After the Red Rain*, the I Hunt Killers trilogy, and his debut, *The Astonishing Adventures of Fanboy and Goth Girl*. Barry lives and writes in New Jersey.

READER DISCUSSION QUESTIONS

I KNOW WHAT YOU DID LAST SUMMER

By Lois Duncan

Prepared by Jeremy Cesarec

1. Early in the book, Julie's mom tells her, "I've never seen such a change in anybody" (p. 2). Her suspicion that something serious has happened turns out to be right. Do you think parents sometimes have special insight? Is there someone in your life who is unusually perceptive?

2. After Julie first reads the fateful note, she tries to stay calm and convince herself it's just a bad dream. Have you ever wished that a really bad experience was actually a nightmare? Why do you think people do that?

3. The friends put a lot of trust in each other when they make the pact—and Barry surely has the most to lose if someone finds out the truth. If you were in Barry's place, would you trust your friends to keep such a serious secret? Are some of your friends more trustworthy than others? Are you good at keeping secrets?

4. When Barry first finds out about Julie's note, he suggests that the girls are overreacting. When he gets a little nervous, he even says to himself, "I'm as uptight as those crazy girls" (p. 21). Do the girls seem to be acting crazy to

you, or are they being reasonable considering the circumstances? Do you find Barry's remark to be sexist?

5. Each of the kids has a different idea of what to do after the accident happens, but Barry is the most persuasive. What is it about Barry that makes him such a leader? Do you know people like him?

6. After the accident, Julie argues that "It's not what we want to do. It's what we have to do. It's the law" (p. 49). Do you agree that when something is the right (or legal) thing to do, you *have* to do it? Why or why not?

7. Barry, Julie, Ray and Helen all seem to have specific expectations from their families that influence their thoughts and behavior. Which of them is most influenced by family pressures? Explain.

8. One theme that comes up throughout the book is the idea of "student unrest," protests and friction about war. Have you ever been involved in any protests? Do you think civil disobedience is powerful and effective?

9. A lot of different elements led to Daniel's death. Do you think Barry is most responsible? Is Daniel's mom responsible in some way for not picking him up from his friend's house? Can more than one person be responsible for a tragic event? Why do you think this?

10. There's a saying that "The eyes are the window to the soul." The author makes a point of commenting several times on how Julie's eyes have seemed to change since the accident. Why do eyes reveal so much about a person?

For a complete Reader's Guide, visit www.LBYR.com.

Turn the page for a preview of

Revenge is a deadly lesson.

KILLING MR. GRIFFIN

BESTSELLING AUTHOR OF *I KNOW WHAT YOU DID LAST SUMMER*

LOIS DUNCAN

AVAILABLE NOW

CHAPTER 1

It was a wild, windy, southwestern spring when the idea of killing Mr. Griffin occurred to them.

As she crossed the playing field to reach the school building, Susan McConnell leaned into the wind and cupped her hands around the edges of her glasses to keep the blowing red dust from filling her eyes. Tumbleweeds swept past her like small, furry animals, rushing to pile in drifts against the fence that separated the field from the parking lot. The parked cars all had their windows up as though against a rainstorm. In the distance, the rugged Sandia Mountains rose in faint outline, almost obscured by the pinkish haze.

I hate spring, Susan told herself vehemently. *I hate dust and wind. I wish we lived somewhere else. Someday —*

It was a word she used often—someday.

"Someday," she had said at the breakfast table that very morning, "someday I'm going to live in a cabin on the shore of a lake where everything is peaceful and green and the only sound is lapping water."

As soon as the words were out she had longed to snatch them back again.

"How are you going to pay the property taxes?" her father had asked in his usual reasonable way. "Lakeshore property doesn't come cheap, you know. Somebody's going to have to finance that lovely green nest of yours."

"A rich husband!" her brother Craig had shouted, and the twins, who were seven, had broken into jeers and laughter.

"Not too soon, I hope," her mother had said, turning from the stove with the frying pan in her hand. "Marry in haste, repent at leisure. That's what my grandmother always said. There's plenty of time for everything."

"For being an old maid?" the twin named Kevin had offered, giggling.

"Don't be ridiculous," Mrs. McConnell had told him. "Nobody is ever an old maid these days. The term is 'single person.' Now, who wants eggs?"

Someday, Susan had thought, sinking lower in her chair, *someday I am going to move out of this house and away from this family. I'll live all alone in a place where I can read and write and think, and the only time I'll ever come here is for Christmas.*

"Are you going to be a single person, Sue?" the twin named Alex had asked with false innocence, jabbing his brother with his elbow, and Craig had grinned with maddening twelve-year-old self-assurance and said, "You've got to go out on dates before you get married, and Sue hasn't even started that yet."

"All things in good time," Mrs. McConnell had told them mildly, and Mr. McConnell had said, "Speaking of property taxes—" and they had been off on another subject.

And Susan, with her eyes on her plate, had told herself silently, *someday—someday—*

The dust stung the sides of her face, filling her nose and coating her lips. With a whir and a flutter, half a dozen sheets of notebook paper went flying past her like strange, white birds released suddenly from the confinement of their cage.

"Grab them!" somebody shouted. "Get them before they go over the fence!"

Susan turned to see David Ruggles running toward her, the slightness and delicacy of his bone structure giving him the framework of a kite with his blue Windbreaker billowing out beneath his arms, the wind seeming to lift and carry him. He sailed by her, grabbing frantically for the escaping papers, and Susan dropped her hands from their protective encasement of her glasses and snatched wildly at the air.

The paper she was trying for lurched suddenly to the ground in front of her, and her foot came down upon it, grinding it into the dirt. Susan stooped and snatched it up.

"It's torn!" The dirty imprint of her shoe was stamped irrevocably in its center. "I'm sorry."

"It doesn't matter." David shrugged his shoulders and reached to take the paper from her hand. "The rest of it's blown away anyhow. One ripped page isn't going to make any difference. If it's not all there, Griffin won't take any of it."

"Is it a song for Ophelia?"

"Yeah. It's supposed to be, but I'm sure Griffin would have called it something else. I haven't done anything right for him yet."

"Neither have I. I don't think anyone has." Susan fell into step beside him, her heart lifting suddenly, her depression disappearing. The wind wasn't so bad after all, for it had blown this luck upon her, the unbelievable, undreamed-of event of herself, Susan McConnell, entering the halls of Del Norte High School side by side with beautiful, popular David Ruggles, president of the senior class.

For the last year of her life, Susan had dreamed about David every night, at least every night in which she could remember having a dream. In some of the dreams he smiled at her, the open, sweet, heart-clenching smile that belonged to him alone. In others they sat and talked for hour after hour, sharing with each other private thoughts and longings. Never yet had there been a dream in which they walked shoulder to shoulder into English class with everyone, even Betsy Cline, turning to stare, to envy, to wonder.

When they reached the door to the building, David struggled with it, pulling with all the weight of his slight frame as the wind forced it closed. For a moment it seemed it would be a draw, but in the end David won, and he and Susan staggered into the crowded hallway where numerous other red-faced, wind-torn students laughed, jostled, shoved tangled hair out of their faces and shouted things like, "So much for my hair!" and "Look what the wind just blew in!"

Susan took off her glasses and wiped the dust from the lenses with the front of her blouse. By the time she put them back on, David had moved away from her. She started to press forward to regain her place beside him, but others had already fallen into it. Mark Kinney: lean, expressionless, cool. Jeff Garrett: big, loud, broad-shouldered.

"Hey, Dave, where were you last night, man?" Jeff asked. "We looked for you after the game."

"I had to miss it. Sorry. Three hours' worth of homework."

"Two of them for Griffin's class, I'll bet."

"A lot of good it did me. Whole stupid assignment blew out of my hands on the way in here—"

They were too far ahead of her now for her to hear them, and Susan accepted defeat. It didn't really matter anyway. Walking into class beside David Ruggles would have been a farce and everyone would have known it. Another girl might have pulled it off, someone with more sophistication than she, someone used to walking beside attractive boys and chatting gaily and smiling disarmingly. The only attractive boys Susan ever walked beside were named McConnell, and most of the time she hated all three of them.

Oh, well, she thought wryly, *at least I stepped on his paper.* That's more than has ever happened before. *Next time we meet he'll know who I am — the girl with the dirty shoes.* Alex's question came back to her—"Are you going to be a single person, Sue?" *No. Yes. Probably*—wasn't that an appropriate fate for someone like Susan McConnell? Someone with a handsome father and a gorgeous, vivacious mother, whose looks had all been poured into three dreadful, handsome, smart-ass little boys? But that was for now. Things did sometimes change. *Someday*—Someday, what? Her boniness would blossom into curves? She would get contact lenses? She who had been told by not one, not two, but three different doctors that her corneas weren't shaped right to allow her to wear them? Someday she would turn into a heart-stopping beauty overnight? Is that what would happen?

Why did she keep trying to fool herself by thinking "someday" when the word was actually "never"?

Morosely, Susan let the tide of bodies sweep her on down the hall and to the door of Room 117. She paused in the doorway long enough to glance about the room. The boys were there ahead of her, David already in his accustomed seat, three from the back in the fifth row, Jeff blocking the center aisle as he stood by Mark's desk, continuing their conversation.

In the seat in front of David, Betsy Cline turned and said

something in a low-pitched, conspiratorial manner. David smiled and nodded.

Sure that she would be unable to wedge herself past Jeff and too shy to ask him to move, Susan entered the room along the side aisle in order to approach her desk from the opposite direction. She smiled tentatively at two girls in the front of the row, but they were talking to each other and did not seem to notice her, so she let her eyes shift away from them and clung tightly to the smile, as though it had not been for them at all but for some private joke that had come suddenly into her mind. She smiled all the way up the aisle, only letting her face relax when she had slipped into her seat.

She glanced up at the wall clock at the front of the room. Two minutes to nine. Two minutes for friends to chatter to each other while Susan stared at her desktop.

Why was it that some people — girls like Betsy, for instance — were noticed and spoken to and appreciated without ever making the slightest effort? It was not all looks, certainly. When you analyzed Betsy, she was not really pretty — she had a round, snub-nosed, pussycat face and short, muscular, cheerleader legs and a sprinkling of freckles. But ask anyone, even the newest of the freshmen, "Who is that girl over there?" and the answer you got would be, "That's Betsy Cline. Doesn't everyone know her?"

The large hand on the wall clock snapped forward with an inaudible click. One minute now until class time. Susan opened her purse and rummaged through it, pretending to be looking for something important. It was easier than simply sitting or than trying again with the smile routine. In other classes it was not quite as difficult. For one thing, she was a straight-A student and people had questions to ask her about homework. Here, in English Literature and Composition, there was no such thing as an A student. With all her effort she was earning B's. Even so, it was more than most of the other students were getting. The mid-semester exam had been a disaster for everyone, and it was rumored that the final was being constructed so that it would be impossible for even the brightest student to pass.

"Griffin must be lying awake at night," Jeff Garrett had commented yesterday in the cafeteria. "He's trying to think of questions that don't have answers." His voice had rung through the room, and everyone had started laughing, knowing whom he was talking about, even if they had missed hearing the name.

Susan dug into the open purse and drew out a felt pen, a stick of gum, a dime and two pennies. She examined them with affected interest before letting them fall back again.

The hand of the clock moved forward one final click. The bell rang. And Mr. Griffin stepped through the doorway into the classroom, pulling the door shut behind him.

The day had officially begun.

Never once could Susan recall a morning when Mr. Griffin had not been there standing in front of them at the precise moment the bell stopped ringing. Other teachers might saunter in late, delayed in the teachers' lounge for a last drag on a cigarette or a final swallow of morning coffee. Other teachers might pause in the hall to secure a button or tie a shoestring. Other teachers might sometimes not appear at all while unorganized substitutes stumbled over their lesson plans and finally gave up and let everybody out early.

But Mr. Griffin was always there, as reliable as the bell itself, stiff and straight in a navy blue suit, white shirt and tie, his dark hair slicked flat against his head, his mouth firm and uncompromising beneath the small, neatly trimmed mustache.

His eyes moved steadily up and down the rows, taking a silent roll call as the buzz of conversation dwindled and faded to silence.

"Good morning, class," he said.

Susan answered automatically, her voice joining the uneasy chorus.

"Good morning, Mr. Griffin."

"Please take out your homework assignments and pass them to the front. Miss Cline, will you collect them, please?"

Susan opened her folder and withdrew the sheets of paper on which she had printed the verses she had composed the night before.

In the seat behind her, Jeff raised his hand.

"Mr. Garrett?"

"I don't have mine finished yet, Mr. Griffin. There was a basketball game last night, and I was one of the starters."

"That must have created a great problem for you, Mr. Garrett."

"I couldn't very well skip the game, could I?" Jeff said. "The team was counting on me. We were playing Eldorado."

"Basketball is indeed an important reason for attending high school," Mr. Griffin said in an expressionless voice. "The ability to drop balls through baskets will serve you well in life. It may keep your wrists limber into old age.

"Mr. Ruggles, your hand is raised. Do you have a similar disclosure to make?"

"I did the assignment, sir," David said. "It blew out of my notebook. I'll redo it tonight."

"I have never accepted late papers on windy days. Miss Cline?"

"I didn't understand the assignment," Betsy said. Her eyes were wide and worried. "How can anybody write a final song for Ophelia when she's already said everything there is to say? All that about rosemary being for remembrance and everything? Nothing happens to her after that except she drowns."

"There are those who might consider suicide an event of some importance in a young woman's life," Mr. Griffin said drily. "Are there any other comments?" The room was silent. "Then will those of you who were able to find some final words for poor Ophelia please pass them forward?"

At least we don't have to read them aloud, Susan thought in relief. That was a possibility she had not thought about last night when she sat at the desk in her room, letting the words pour from her. There, caught by the magic of the painful story, she had let herself become Ophelia—lonely, alienated from the world, sickened with the hopelessness of her love, gazing into the depths of the water that would soon become her grave.

Only this morning, as she was leaving the house, had the horrible thought occurred to her— *What if he makes us read the songs in class?* There was no way that she could have done that. Too much of Susan lay exposed in the neatly printed verses, intermixed with the persona of Ophelia.

Now she scanned her words again—

Where the daisies laugh and blow,
Where the willow leaves hang down,
Nonny, nonny, I will go
There to weave my lord a crown.

Willow, willow, by the brook,
Trailing fingers green and long,
I will read my lord a book,
I will sing my love a song.

Though he turn his face away,
Nonny, nonny, still I sing,
Ditties of a heart gone gray
And a hand that bears no ring.

Water, water, cold and deep —

"Miss McConnell, have you completed your meditation?" Mr. Griffin's voice broke in upon her.

"I'm sorry." Susan felt her face growing hot with embarrassment. "I was just—just—checking the spelling." Hurriedly she thrust the papers into the hand of the girl in front of her.

"An excellent idea, but it might have been done before now. As for those who have no paper to turn in, you may consider your grade an F for this assignment. Now, open your books, please, to the first scene in Act Three."

"But, Mr. Griffin, that's not fair!" Jeff burst out. "If we missed doing the assignment we should be allowed to do a makeup!"

"Why is that, Mr. Garrett?"

"Other teachers take late papers!" Jeff said. "In fact, most teachers don't give assignments at all on game nights. Dolly Luna—"

"What Miss Luna does is no concern of mine. She teaches her class according to her policies," Mr. Griffin told him. "My own policy happens to be to teach English literature. If students wish to take part in extracurricular activities, that's fine, but they should be just that—extra. Any student who allows them to interfere with his academic responsibilities must be prepared to accept the consequences."

"And the consequences are F's, is that it?" Jeff's voice was shaking with outrage. "Well, there happen to be a lot of us who think there's more to life than trying to outdo Shakespeare!

When we do turn stuff in, it comes back so marked up that nobody can read it. Spelling, grammar, punctuation—everything's got to be so freaking perfect—"

"Cool it," Mark Kinney said quietly. He sat slouched in his seat in his usual don't-care position, his odd, heavy-lidded eyes giving him a deceptively sleepy appearance. "Jeff's sort of overexcited, Mr. G., but what he's getting at is that most of us are seniors in this class. We need this credit to graduate."

"We sure do!" Jeff sputtered. "By handing F's out whole-sale, you may be knocking a bunch of us out of graduation. It's not fair to us or to our parents or even to the school! What are they going to do next fall with twenty or so of us all back trying to get one lousy English credit?!"

"It's interesting to contemplate, isn't it?" Mr. Griffin said mildly. "But I'd advise you not to be lulled into a false sense of security by the thought that it can't be done. I am quite capable of holding back anyone I feel has not qualified for a passing grade, a fact which your friend Mr. Kinney can support."

His hand slid into his jacket pocket and brought out a small, plastic bottle. Without seeming to so much as glance at it, he snapped it open, took out a pill, and popped it into his mouth. Then he recapped the bottle and placed it back in the pocket.

"Please, open your books to *Hamlet*, Act Three, Scene One. We'll now review for a quiz I have scheduled for Monday. You do have your book with you, don't you, Mr. Garrett?"

"Yes, I do—sir," Jeff said hoarsely.

The wind continued to blow. Gazing through the window toward the parking lot, Susan could barely make out the rows of cars, veiled as they were by swirling dust. Out of this wild, pink world a bird came flying, half-blinded, carried by the wind, and crashed headlong into the windowpane. Its beak crumpled against the glass, and it seemed to hang there an instant, stunned by the impact, before it dropped like a feather-covered stone to the ground below.

Poor thing, Susan thought. *Poor little thing.* Poor bird. Poor Ophelia. Poor Susan. She had a sudden, irrational urge to put her head down on the desk and weep for all of them, for the whole world, for the awful day that was starting so badly and would certainly get no better.

From his seat behind her she heard Jeff Garrett mumble under his breath, "That Griffin's the sort of guy you'd like to kill."

Lois Duncan

was born in Philadelphia, Pennsylvania, and grew up in Sarasota, Florida. She knew from early childhood that she wanted to be a writer. She submitted her first story to a magazine at age ten and became published at thirteen. Throughout her high school years she wrote regularly for young people's publications, particularly *Seventeen*.

Nine of her novels—including *Summer of Fear, Killing Mr. Griffin, Gallows Hill, Ransom, Don't Look Behind You, Stranger with My Face,* and *Down a Dark Hall*—were made into movies. *I Know What You Did Last Summer* and *Hotel for Dogs* were box office hits.

Lois was the author of over fifty books, ranging from children's picture books to poetry to adult nonfiction, but is best known for her young adult suspense novels.

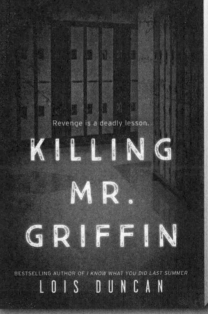